A PLA
BETWEEN THE
MOUNTAINS

PAUL C.WALSH

Thanks Sue

*for all your
patient reading
of the text
(& the typos)*

X Paul

APS PUBLICATIONS

A catalogue record for this book is available from the British Library

ISBN 9781912309511

APS Publications, 4 Oakleigh Road, Stourbridge, West Midlands, DY8 2JX

www.andrewsparke.com

When the metal bird flies and the horses roll on wheels, the Tibetans will be scattered about the world and the Dharma of the Buddha will reach the farthest countries.

(Prophecy of Padmasambhava, 8th Century)

PART ONE

AN INVITATION

1

Recollections from the past

Luke put the phone down and mumbled, profanely, to himself. A meaningless gesture, to soothe his anger. It hadn't worked. It rarely did. He found it difficult to talk to Debbie these days, especially when she was reminding him of his failings. That seemed to happen most of the time she rang! He knew the mere sound of her voice was enough to trigger such a reaction. It brought back unhappy memories of the final months of an all too brief marriage. It hadn't even lasted long enough to celebrate the third anniversary party he had surreptitiously planned. He remembered the surprise, the embarrassment, the utter humiliation of it all. How did he not see that she was about to walk away? His clumsy efforts to rescind the party invitations only enhanced the tragedy, played out before a social circle of knowing whispers. If there had been someone else in the room at that very moment, he would have unleashed his tirade of frustrations in their direction. Instead, he closed his eyes and longed for the presence of a sympathetic ear. Hers. But there wasn't anyone there. Not anymore. Just him, alone with his irritations, about a woman he still loved.

He looked across at his computer screen. If he'd done what he said he was going to do, then she wouldn't have called. But it was now Monday and he hadn't got around to it yet. Guilty as charged, once again! His reluctance on this occasion, was fuelled by one of his biggest gripes about modern life: social media. More specifically, he had never been much of a fan of *Facebook*. Casting his mind back to 2006, he remembered watching reports of it on TV, mushrooming from an unknown student flat at Harvard University, in the States. Some guy called Zuckerberg, he recalled.

'It will fizzle out', Luke had pronounced confidently, at the time. Not his most impressive prediction, he had to admit! But despite its global impact, he still wasn't convinced about its claims. Yes, he'd been persuaded to open a *Facebook* account, but he hardly ever logged on to it. Luke didn't need another panacea for global networking, or a window-box to discover new friends and contacts. It was changing the way people communicated and he didn't like it! Whether used as a public photo store for the world to gaze in at their children, their friends or holiday experiences; or an on-line cocoon from which to climb out and share all that endless, meaningless daily drivel that's best left to ossify in one's head: it wasn't for him. He wouldn't even begin to touch upon those who used it as a platform to proclaim their radical political or religious truths.

And it wasn't just *Facebook* that Luke thought was turning people into self-obsessed 'china dolls'.

The sound of boiling water from the kitchen, distracted him for a few moments. But the kettle had only paused his train of thought. Sipping his mug of tea, he wondered why so many pursued a frenzied need to be *liked* by complete strangers, or sometimes appearing to fall apart, if they didn't receive the sort of un-critical attention they craved for?'

His brain was now bursting with 'cyber- resistance.' His angst, his prejudices, in full flow. *Twitter, Instagram,* Mm. He could go on. He often did. Debbie used to say so. His rant continued with its usual hint of subliminal arrogance. 'Wasn't it just religious leaders, politicians, musicians or famous sports teams who were supposed to have *followers?*

Maybe, he thought, he was as guilty as everyone else, in helping to maintain this illusionary world. An occasional voyeur, drawn by morbid fascination to what occupied the minds of some he purported to know. Yes, Luke approached the wonders of cyber-life with some trepidation. Too often, he was left with the numbness of uncertainty. He was convinced that people shared on-line, just a little too much of themselves open to public scrutiny. A multitude of insecure souls who were desperate for people to listen to them; unknowingly enslaved by the therapeutic enticements of their digital world.

Not for the first time, he knew he'd plunged, un-controllably, into another of his tedious, internal rambles. Luke had to admit to himself, that sometimes, it felt like he was being dragged screaming and kicking into some sort of dystopian nightmare! He stared across the room in the direction of the empty armchair. If only, his confidante had stayed. She was so much more than a partner.

He didn't seem to have many friends, anymore. Those he had, would need to have the patience of Job!' His mind eventually drifted back to the reason he'd become preoccupied with *Facebook*. An eight- year old girl's holiday pictures. Not any little girl. His pride and joy. His only daughter.

Despite the cynicism fixed firmly in his head, a rare excursion to his least favourite social network site, had brought something unusual to Luke's attention. Having just completed a sales report for his boss, Martin Thomas, and with twenty minutes to spare before lunch, he remembered a promise he'd made on the phone, that Friday evening. His daughter, Ellen, had rang to tell him about her weekend on the Devon coast with her mum, Debbie. 'Make sure you check out the pictures, Dad!' He felt somewhat obliged. Not just because he was her father. It was Luke who'd bought the camera for her recent eighth birthday.

Maybe he was looking for a distraction from work. Maybe, he realised that three days was long enough, if not a lifetime, for any eight-year old to wait for a response. He clicked on to Debbie's *Facebook* page and looked at the photos. The sight of almost fifty, seemingly identical images of mum and daughter posing, rather aimlessly on the beach, aggravated him. An understandable reaction. Luke desperately wanted to be there, sharing such moments with them, not observing the memory from a computer screen. Once upon a time he would have been. Not now. Just fortnightly visits, wrapped around days out, topped up with entertainment and fast food.

Luke's eyes had drifted across to the computer 'messages' bar. He wondered, years later, why he chose to look at his e-mails at that precise moment. Maybe it was fate. There was a new communication. He almost deleted it, but something prevented him from consigning this one to cyber oblivion. He opened the link and found the following:

'This is a message for you Luke and I think it might help to change your life. Remember me? Alan! I've been living overseas for several years now and I've discovered something I want to share with you all. Oh, and by the way, just to let you know, I am not trying to sell you anything! On the contrary, it's a free invitation, with no cost to any of you. It would be good to speak again after all these years. However, if you are completely content with your life as it is, feel free to ignore this. I won't be offended. People move on. But maybe, you are curious enough to find out more. If so, please call me on this number. It would be great to hear from you again'

Luke's immediate reaction was defensive. Was he was being enticed into the world of the weird and the wacky; those legions of quasi-religious groups that operate in this territory? Maybe, this was another of those evangelical faith groups with membership problems? Or was it an attempt to sell him obscure literature to aid his personal salvation, or just another company with an expensive 'app' to peddle? The Alan he recalled wouldn't have fitted naturally into any of these categories.

However, alongside this message was something that triggered a memory flash. It was signed 'the sleeper.' His mind was immediately transported back, more than a decade, to the middle 2000's. He was thinking about a squalid student flat in West London, where he once lived. Back, on the other side of the Atlantic, Zukerberg and his friends had just identified the embryo of a life -changing idea for millions of people. There were less dramatic events occurring at his old place, in the leafy suburbs of West London. But the significance of the individuals he lived with and befriended, would never be forgotten. He closed his eyes, again. He could see him there. Spread-eagled across a badly stained and threadbare brown sofa. Alan, his flatmate, his friend. It had been Luke who had nicknamed him the 'sleeper'. The rest of them soon adopted the name.

In total, six of them had moved in to share the accommodation. Everyone who knew him, thought they had the measure of Alan. If any image captured the personality of the man, it was this picture of prostrate contentedness. Luke's recollections continued to flood back. Always claiming to be deep in thought, was Alan, and doing much of his thinking on that filthy old sofa.

He often said that one day he would have such an idea that it would rip through his head like a sandstorm across an empty desert. Everyone would see it; be astounded. They all laughed. The couch was his territory, his podium and he was free to elucidate his grand schemes to the bugs that no doubt, lived beneath his philosophical throne. Nobody else was really listening.

To the rest of them, Alan's proclamations seemed to be caught within a 'groundhog-day' loop of endless disappointments. He was trapped, it seems, in a repetition of ill-conceived and incomplete dreams. Sadly, his new friends at the house also came to realise this about Alan: that there was never any substance to his ideas. They fizzled away, just like his once promising academic potential.

At least, some of his thinking should have found its way into the coursework assignments that he, like the rest of them, was required to complete. They had tried to help him get to grips with these assessments. Sarah had even risked falling foul of the plagiarism board by drafting his last couple of essays, for him. By the time he'd failed his second year at university, again, they all knew that the writing was on the wall for Alan. There would be no additional re-sit year. There were no 'mitigating circumstances', as the official letter bluntly explained. Although he stayed on at the flat for a while, working at the university bar, he eventually left in June. Luke could vividly remember the day Alan left. The awkward farewells and half-hearted promises to keep in touch. Most of all he recalled the look of loss on Alan's face. He seemed to be struggling to hold back the tears. That was almost eleven years ago. Nobody had heard from him since.

Luke sat there, thinking about the message. He was fermenting waves of random images. What did Alan mean by 'contentedness', when his mobile rang.

Saul was as ebullient, as ever. 'John, boy! You, old fart! How's it going?' (He hardly ever called Luke by his real name)

'Not bad, mate. You still chasing after that nurse in Ealing?'

6

If there was one thing to bring Saul back to earth, it was his spectacular lack of long-term success with female partners.

'It was going so well and then she suddenly ditched me for a fucking accountant in Richmond!'

Luke chuckled but guessed what was coming next.

'Her loss and anyway, I've met someone new'.

'You must be close to running out of local choices, my friend, with your extensive track record!'

Saul cleared his throat and immediately got to the point.

'I know you're a bit of a luddite, mate, when it comes to *social media*, but I received an unusual message on *Facebook* yesterday which may interest you. From somebody we haven't heard from, in a very long time.'

The mention of Alan's name made Luke feel a little uneasy. He said nonchalantly, 'Oh yes, from Alan Rogers. I've seen it.'

Saul was surprised that his social media shy friend had already picked up the communication. 'You've been on *Facebook*?' His voice carried an irritatingly mocking tone.

'Yes, funnily, I have. Keeping a promise to my daughter'.

'And so, have all the others, it seems', Saul interrupted.

Once Luke eliminated the bizarre notion that his former flat-mates were all fulfilling promises to his daughter, he remembered the line in the message: *With no cost to any of you*.

Saul continued. 'You remember that old house we shared at university for a couple of years?'

Luke needed no reminders. Glimpses of a forgotten age continued to creep back into his head. Saul was the only one of his former flat-mates that Luke was still in contact with. The 'others' were a mixed group of diverse characters, bound together by memories of university life; that stained brown sofa and the other faded furnishings and fittings that belonged to 105, Weston Road, Ealing. A less than salubrious property, but home for six, young undergraduates at Middlesex University. With the exception, of Saul, Luke realised that he hadn't thought about any of the others for some considerable time.

2

New Faces

One of those house-mates was 'Mo' or Mohammed Al-Hazith, as the college register (and his family) knew him. When his new flatmates first met him, Mohammed thought, rather naively, that they'd be impressed by the grandeur of his name. Having two first names which were identical was surely striking. Especially when that was the name of the holy prophet of Islam. The other male occupants of the house, including Luke, didn't quite see it that way. They thought it was hilarious.

Mo quickly got used to his new house-name and his flatmate's constant ribbing, together with the lampooning of several other traits, mostly linked to his Muslim identity. 'We are all under the gaze of Allah!' was one of his favourite phrases. Luke and Saul started to use it as an alternative greeting to good morning, when they bumped into him. The response of three, largely ignorant white Caucasian atheists, was to constantly probe for material to use against him, albeit, in light-hearted jest; filling regular moments of idleness with comic indifference. Luke wasn't sure why Mo put up with it and stayed. But he did.

Sarah and Gurdeep, on the other hand, were far more sensitive to the value that some of their contemporaries placed upon religious identity. They tried to keep the rest of the household in check. In those days, the lads labelled it humour. How different things are now. Luke cringed as he thought about what modern sensibilities would make of such behaviour but much of what was delivered towards Mo then, was considered by the guys as no more than good-natured banter.

As the months went by, the flat-mates, grew to really like Mohammed. There was more than a little fascination, even a touch of un-spoken admiration, woven into this lampooning of their new Islamic friend, as they referred to him. In truth, none of the guys had known any Muslim families before and what little knowledge of Islam they had picked up, was packaged around negative, sensationalised stories in the tabloid press. What they began to realise, was that Mo was quite a sensitive and considerate young man with a real sense of dedication to his faith. He had a gift for peeling away the stereotypes that people like them, indulged in, mercilessly. Always delivered, without bitterness or anger. He understood they didn't mean anything by it. They admired that about him. But they knew little of the secret that Mo screened away from the world.

Luke pictured the faces of the other members of the house who contributed to their emerging multi- religious and cultural understanding of West London life.

Saul was quintessentially Jewish. It wasn't difficult to guess his ethnic origins. Symbolic clues adorned both his bed-room walls and his daily rhetoric. Tall, handsome, opinionated and blessed with the persuasive skills of a successful politician, Saul simply oozed confidence. He was particularly keen to communicate to all that his allegiances to Judaism lay within the Progressive, rather than the Orthodox ideology. Not that any of the lads understood the difference. They did, however, formulate their own theory. They suspected that his choice may have been a pragmatic decision, based upon the limited choice of prospective girlfriends around his family synagogue community in Mill Hill. His mother, he informed them, had finally despaired of him when he started dating a black Caribbean singer that he met in a local night-club. His Mum had begun to realize the futility of her maternal dream. Her only son was unlikely to settle down with an Orthodox Jewish spouse, despite her considerable efforts to provide the opportunities. This Orthodox family-line would not be extended any further by Saul, at least not in traditional religious terms. The rest of the flat-mates responded with some bewilderment, as marrying a non-Orthodox girl was extremely low on the list of serious 'transgressions' they managed to come up with. Sarah was aghast and reeled off three examples of debauched or illegal behaviour, or, in some cases, both, that she had indulged in during her self-proclaimed wild period of late teenage indulgence. It was one of the few times that the boys sat quietly; frozen with licentious fascination.

Gurdeep was different. She had grown up in the Punjabi region of India. She was also a Sikh. A little older than the rest of them, she initially came across as rather shy and a little cautious. Beneath the surface, the rest of them sensed that a powerful sadness had gripped her. They guessed some tragedy had visited her in the past. There seemed to be a fear, an anxiety, born of great trauma, that limited the degree of happiness she could muster in any one day, even though she gave the impression of trying to combat this. Like some weighty, melancholic yoke, it had crushed her spirit and carved marks of anxiety across the contours of her face. Whatever this burden was, it seemed to have spread a shadow over her, prematurely darkened her eyes and aging her features. She never spoke about what had happened to her and they learned it was best not to ask. At the time, they were far more interested in her culinary skills. When she offered to cook for the rest of them, it was worth staying around. Her north Indian cuisine bewitched the taste-buds of hungry young students who largely survived on a mixed diet of trusted and cheap student meals like beans on toast. It was so delicious that Saul had even offered to wash up afterwards in a rare gesture of domestic responsibility.

Gurdeep was also the most studious of all of them. The demands of her Chemistry degree seemed to take up most of her time. They learned from her, that there was a world of difference between choosing a couple of prescribed texts to gain an overview of a topic and completing most of the reading from an extended reading list. This may have seemed obvious to more conscientious students but eluded the immature minds of those whose focus lay elsewhere. This partly explained the fact that Gurdeep had little time or inclination for hanging out with them, socially. When she wasn't studying, she could be found working at the local supermarket, just around the corner from the house. She had hinted that money was in short supply. Together with her strict aversion to alcohol, this kept her apart from their nocturnal student activities and reinforced a choice for academic work over late- night socialising.

They were initially quite surprised when Gurdeep answered the advert to join them at the house. A mix-up at the accommodation centre had led her having to make an emergency decision. They remembered, how she arrived; flustered and, after meeting Alan and Saul, far from convinced that the boisterous atmosphere in the house was what she was looking for. 'I'll see how I get on this month', was her cautious comment on the day she came to look around the property. She ended up staying two years until they all went their separate ways after graduation, in 2009. The last Saul or Luke heard about Gurdeep, she was working for a large pharmaceutical firm, somewhere in London.

Sarah certainly didn't fit such a profile. She was all Gaelic mist and dragon fire. A melting pot of emotions and reactions, driven by a compassionate Irish heart. Nothing was too much trouble for this servant of good causes, but woe-betide anyone who outraged the commitment to justice that she carried around with her, worn like a badge of honour. Sarah was a woman born to carry a banner for *Human Rights*, wherever she perceived them to be at risk. Her Catholic background, ingrained with all its layers of certainty about faith and values, had slowly given way to a philosophical curiosity about other religions. She became close to Gurdeep and Mo and was keen to embroil her cultural outlook with ideas drawn from the cultures of Islam and Sikhism. The other thing that people couldn't help but notice about Sarah, was her passion for alcohol. This allowed her to act as a perfect bridge at the flat, connecting the contemplative to the secular; keeping communication lines open when tensions arose between members of the house. She had done much of the initial paperwork in securing the accommodation and the tricky task of filling the vacant rooms quickly. With hindsight, it might have been better to find out a little more about the personalities who were about to join her in these living arrangements. After all, they could hardly be described as a harmonious group. But Sarah addressed this task with all the gusto of a woman driven by the urgency of expediency. The next challenge was no less difficult: trying to dove-tail them into some loose sort of functioning domestic unit. It would take attitudes and habits that were initially in short supply among some of the other flatmates in those carefree, halcyon days of youth.

This band of insecure young fledglings, most of them recently released from the constraints of parental influence, were just trying to set up a temporary home together. It was an understatement to say that some of them were oblivious to the practical implications of such a venture. In theory, bonded by a common desire to create something of a base for their emerging adult lives, the reality was rather simpler. They were all just stumbling, step by step, into adulthood. Living in halls for the first year, had only delayed them facing up to the many of the implications of being a grown up. Thank God for the moderating influences of Mo and Gurdeep, Luke had observed at the time.

And what of Luke? He once heard someone say that it can be a humbling process to analyse the missed opportunities and unfulfilled hopes that lie, scattered across the pages of one's early adult life. The person was talking about Alan. But these words had stuck a note with him, too. He was just being honest. It described him perfectly. He might have added that if we're not careful, we can easily drift through these formative years, until one day, we realise that all those plans and hopes for the future have suffocated under the day-to-day expediencies of survival. The disappointments and setbacks, then become the experiences we think most about, rather than the joys and achievements that have come our way. Pragmatism and cynicism start to grow deep roots. This encapsulated Luke's view of himself. If he died tomorrow, it would provide a fitting epitaph. 'Here lies a man who tried to succeed in many things. But life didn't quite work out for him!'

He didn't need anyone to tell him how little he had developed in the decade that had passed by. Luke knew that many, like him, stand waiting for things to change. Or, for somebody to change them for him. But sometimes, it takes a monumental event to fracture such lethargy. When it happens, your world can be turned completely upside down. What Luke did learn was that if fate conjures up such a moment, it is better not to know the hour nor the circumstances. Rather like dealing with death. It will often be the most traumatic experience of your life. It was for him.

3

Lost Opportunities

Back in 2009, Luke thought he was ready for his metamorphosis into the world of work. Armed, somewhat fortuitously, with a 2:1 degree in Business Studies, after his modest efforts at university, and with the promise of a competitive salary, he began work at an artefact import company. Initially, there was much optimism. After all, what could go wrong, he thought?

Saul and Luke had become good friends, after their studies, and a little of his exuberance had rubbed off on Luke. He became, in effect, his social secretary, providing a conveyor-belt of opportunities to enjoy the new lifestyle afforded to young graduates, working in central London. For the first time in their lives, they had money to burn!

Saul was in a similar position, having graduated in Economics and working for a major IT Consultancy group. The proximity of their employments led them to share a small flat together, after they all left Weston Road, in June of that year.

It was through Saul that he met Debbie. Saul had arranged to have a few people around to celebrate his twenty-second birthday and Debbie was there, with her friend Jade. While Jade ingratiated herself into Saul's affections, Luke filled the vacuum created by Debbie's sudden isolation. Despite some initial awkwardness by Luke, most specifically in denying any pre-planned attempts to match them up, they connected well. Luke recalled a familiar image of the day. A feisty young woman, full of life, with beautiful long brown hair, gently cascaded across a slender frame. Quick- witted and confident, too. Those piercing eyes, searching for his reactions to her words and ideas, like a lighthouse beam penetrating the darkness of an early morning mist. When she looked at him, Debbie seemed to gaze into the very depths of his soul. Wow! What had he done to merit this slice of good fortune?

In blissful naivety, he thought all this would never change. That first evening together had drifted away in effortless enjoyment. He was besotted with her, even a little bewildered, that such an experience had occurred, and right in the middle of his own flat. Six months later, they were engaged and, before the end of the following year, married. Saul joked at the time that he'd keep Luke's room vacant. Just in case his friend needed somewhere to stay, when she grew tired of him and kicked him out! They laughed about it at the time. However, those special moments that Debbie and Luke shared in the early days didn't last long. Despite being blessed with the arrival of a daughter, Ellen, a succession of tensions arose and took root. They strangled the early affection; the love that had blossomed between them, until it became impossible to live together any longer. By this time Saul had a new lodger and Luke was in no mood to acknowledge the irony of his friend's prophesy. Nor was the option to return, still available.

Luke had made a conscious effort to get to the supermarket earlier than usual. It was only Friday tea-time, but the rest of the weekend would be his when he got home. His shopping trolley had been hastily filled to the brim with his usual selection of bland food and alcoholic boosts. After what seemed like an eternity, his patient crawl to the front of the check-out was nearing its end. He knew it was a mistake to come there at this time, but he was going out later. He fumbled in his wallet for his debit card. As he waited for the transaction to complete, a photo fell from its protective sleeve in his wallet. It was one of his favourites. Some might call it a 'happy families' snap. A smiling mum, dad and child, cuddled together in a contented embrace. This was a picture of happiness, occupying a special space in his world, where everything looked perfect. Of course, real life is rarely like that and nor was Luke's marriage at the time. The photo, like many parts of his relationship with Debbie, presented a faded image. It too had a shelf-life. Yet, he still liked to be reminded of the fantasy.

Despite an early period of contentment, the tensions between them grew. Debbie was keen to maintain a healthy social life. She said it would keep the 'fires of interest' burning, in the relationship. He never really understood what she meant by this. While Debbie stood at the front door, waiting for her taxi to transport her to her latest engineering project, he was pre-occupied with that other old saying, about *absence making the heart grow fonder*. It did for him. He had hoped she felt the same.

In the early days of their relationship, they would often go out socially together. Sometimes on their own to see a movie, or to watch a band they liked. Occasionally, they were accompanied by Saul and Debbie's friend, Jade. It came as no surprise to anybody, except perhaps Jade, when she was eventually added to Saul's growing list of exes'. Debbie started to prefer the company of her female friends again and Luke ended up spending even more time than he'd anticipated, with Saul. Debbie's work, as an electrical engineer, took her out to several locations, around the region. She was sometimes required to stay overnight. Once the novelty of recognising her success in this, largely male-dominated profession had subsided, he started to resent her lifestyle. It wasn't just jealousy. He was

13

spending too many nights at home, alone, for his own liking. The additional money she brought in was useful, but it didn't compensate for her absence. He was also getting a little fed-up with being a domestic drone. Well, someone needed to keep up with the housework. He wondered what she did on those evenings, away working. Mainly socialising with other men, he concluded. It was obvious. Although, he had never really doubted her loyalty and commitment, his mind had started to play tricks. Maybe, it was because he had so much time on his hands.

Perhaps, he should have invested more time in his own professional development. Luke's career hadn't quite taken off as he had anticipated. Although he tried to show interest in the wider world of artefacts and antiques, he struggled to motivate himself. The glamourous image that had been sold to him at interview, was a far cry from the daily mundane reality he faced. Most of his working hours were spent typing out orders on his computer and chasing up reluctant clients for overdue payments. He completed such tasks, dutifully. He had also formed the impression that his boss was a little disappointed with him; that he thought he had much more to offer.

Not exactly lazy, he had concluded, but more a case of coasting a little too much, at times. Maybe, his boss wanted to see more initiative. Mr Smith had even called him in one day, for a chat about the subject. It was clear to Luke that this was some kind, of veiled warning, even if *Smithy* wasn't that comfortable or lucid, in delivering that sort of thing. In truth, Luke wasn't surprised. He was bored. He realised he should have responded to this by looking around for something different to do, but that would involve moving out of his comfort zone. Not Luke's style. He also knew how transparent he could appear. When he tried to lie, his face would turn crimson. What he didn't always recognise, was how his personality, his indifference, was displayed to the outside world. He had a caring side, but others rarely saw it. This wasn't surprising. There was little evidence that he showed much empathy to those outside his immediate family circle.

Although the people he worked with, tended to respect his knowledge and length of service at the company, they didn't seem that interested in the person that lay underneath. The one exception to this was Leena. She didn't find him dull at all. Leena was often flirtatious around the office and made her intentions rather obvious to Luke. Yes, he started to be a bit suggestive, but it was all in the spirit of office banter. He blamed the influence of Saul for his flippancy, but it wasn't an excuse for the suggestive comments he made to her in the office. He knew that.

Luke wondered how much of all this was down to his early experiences of life at home. More specifically, the thorny subject of his attitude towards his brother,

Ian. His sibling was two years younger, but in terms of his achievements, decades ahead of him. For almost as long, as he could remember, there was this persistent idea in his head that his parents favoured the younger of the two boys. Mum and Dad would have virulently denied it, of course. 'Professional people would never fall into such a parenting trap, would they?' he mused. Whereas, Luke maintained a somewhat pedestrian pace to most of life's endeavours during childhood, Ian stormed ahead, displaying the energy and talents, commensurate with the accomplishments of several children. The older brother's more modest achievements seemed to sink without trace in their eyes, beneath Ian's spectacular success in study and sports. By the time his brother had been picked for county honours in both football and cricket and won maths and science awards at the age of fifteen, Luke had decided that he didn't care much for his family any more. His reasoning was clear; there was little evidence to suggest, that any of them cared for him. Of course, this wasn't true, but it was nevertheless how he saw it. It was a relief to pass his 'A' levels with sufficient grades (just), to take up a place at university. In doing so, he could leave behind the unbridled coronation of his younger brother. With hindsight, he did the right thing. Luke suspected that Ian's status at home, might one day, take a tumble. He didn't expect it to come so soon after he left, via the impregnation of Lucy Phillips, at his local Comprehensive school. Her unwillingness to have an abortion, aided by her family's Christian beliefs, meant Ian had even beaten him, unlikely as it was, in the race to fatherhood. Still, it slowed down the process of beatification, as Mum and Dad faced the awkward reality that their precious little Ian might not be so perfect after all. They could hardly blame the older brother for this one.

Luke had realised that he poured the boiling water into his mug so time ago. His tea was getting cold.

Thinking about Ian's exploits had reminded him about another pregnancy, much closer to his heart. Given the growing tensions around his wife's lifestyle, he was surprised, one November night, when on her return from a working trip to Liverpool, she brought up the subject of babies. To be more precise, her desire to have one and soon. Luke didn't take much persuasion. He'd always wanted to be a dad. It was just the distraction she needed, he thought, to lever her away from regular trips away. After all, these two spheres of life were hardly compatible. She would have to make changes. There would be other advantages, too. Apart from securing her regular companionship, again, he expected motherhood to curtail her professional ambition. At least, in the short term. Furthermore, with Debbie's desire to have a baby, it also occurred to him that his status as a father might help to give him more gravitas with people. Maybe, a more humane persona, at work? Yes! He would be thrilled to be a dad, but he also wanted the rest of the world to respect him for it.

Nine months and two days later, Debbie gave birth to a daughter. It hadn't taken much endeavour, unlike so many couples they knew. One attempt, one child. There were no unexpected dramas, along the way; no miscarriages or illnesses. But everything changed once Ellen arrived. It was Luke though, not his spouse, who struggled to adjust to family life. It wasn't just Debbie who became locked into the endless cycle of feeding, cleaning and planning for Ellen's needs. The idea of breast-feeding was soon abandoned, and Luke became a skilled manager of all things associated with powdered milk.

Sex, however, was another subject! Regular early nights were for catching up with missed sleep, he was told by his partner. Luke thought his sex life resembled a favourite film from the past; rich in well- intended nostalgia but fading with every rare viewing. This lack of sexual activity weighed heavily on Luke's mind. He realised there would initially be less than there had been in the past, but he hadn't counted on quite how little. A combination of a period of post -natal depression, a uterine infection and a general sense of tiredness, reduced Debbie's interest in intimacy. Their conjugal life had been brought to a shuddering halt. He started running, going to the gym, anything to keep those sexual urges at bay, without success. The occasional sympathetic cuddle, in front of the TV, was not enough. He felt the excitement of their relationship, fizzling away. Although he still loved her and beautiful little Ellen, his frustrations were growing.

He knew it was a stupid thing to do. A calamitous mistake! He'd heard so many others joking about the destruction it can cause to a marriage. Luke just couldn't stop himself. Lack of willpower? The discretion was neither satisfying nor memorable. A quick shag after work in the community room. It was all so easy. He had the keys to lock up. Smithy was away in Bristol. Leena was willing. He was initially flattered by her attentions.

He'd thought the flirting was harmless but one night he gave her a lift home, after work, and his inhibitions were cast aside, when an innocuous goodnight kiss turned into something neither of them had anticipated. He ended up leaving the house more than an hour later. It wasn't going to happen again, they agreed, but it did.

Two days later, at the office. Leena had seen Mr Smith giving Luke the keys that morning and asking him to lock up later. His secretary had drifted into Luke's office, on the pretence of returning some company papers. Leena could be very persuasive. She made it clear that some 'extra-curricular' activity, was certainly on the menu that day. They just needed to wait for their colleagues to leave the building. He felt ridiculous afterwards and apologised for his lack of self-control. Leena just laughed. She was a free spirit. But Luke was not. He had a wife and young daughter.

There was only one thing he could do. He was so transparent, anyway. Luke was never going to successfully disguise his infidelity, even if he tried. So, he told Debbie, four days later. Saul had told him not to do it. 'She won't understand, and she won't forgive you. Don't go there, squire', he counselled his friend. The advice was ignored.

Saul's reading of the situation was unnervingly accurate. Debbie went berserk. Once the tears and anger had subsided, bitterness and resentment took over. She shared with him, the details of numerous propositions that had been presented to her, while working away. He cringed as she defiantly explained that she had never succumbed to any of these offers. She was married, relatively happy in her relationship and not available to others. Just as he should have been. 'Leena's flirting should have been brushed off with the contempt it deserved.' She was young, attractive and still honing her seductive skills. There would be lots of suitors for her to practise on. He did not need to be one of them. He was out of bounds; spoken for.

They talked for hours about trust, or the lack of it. How would she ever believe anything he said in the future? She had been betrayed and nothing would be the same again. It was almost a month later that she told him. He would have to move out. There would be no forgiveness. No reconciliation. The marriage was over. He didn't fully realise the implications at the time. It wasn't just the reduced access to his daughter, or the impact of the maintenance payments for Ellen. It wasn't the fact he had to find somewhere else to live, nor the stigma of betrayal he now carried around, with friends and family. He simply missed them both; terribly. Whenever he saw Debbie with another man, he couldn't deal with the unpalatable truth that his crumbling personal life was all down to him. There was nobody else to blame.

There would be little comfort in discovering, later, that each of his former flatmates was also struggling with their own personal challenges.

4

A forgotten friend

Mohammed was the next, to make contact, with the enigmatic Alan. He later reported to the rest of them, a breathless conversation he'd had with him, as Alan described where he was. Himalayan mountains, twisting rivers, where snow and mist merged to bewitch the unsuspecting visitor, all presented a mystical, if not slightly dangerous, picture of his location. There was talk of profound human experiences at the heart of a community made up of many nationalities, bound by Buddhist and Hindu principals and the wisdom of ancient truths. Mohammed later shared all of this with Saul and Luke, but flagging-up some concerns about their former flatmates sanity.

However, other elements of the conversation reminded Mo of stories his grandfather had told him about their family home in the mountains of Pakistan. Living amongst the high peaks was hard, the old man used to say, but people were much more content with their lives than their city relatives. There was a sense of harmony within these isolated villages, partially born from their respect and understanding of the natural elements which influenced their lives so profoundly. The proximity of such natural splendours more than compensated for the lack of affluent excesses enjoyed in urban life. A part of Mohammed had always wanted to visit the Himalaya. He promised to ring again, soon, to let Alan know whether he would be able to take up the invitation. The cautious tone of his voice betrayed the likelihood of a negative answer.

After Mohammed put the phone down, he paused to absorb what he had just heard. This was hardly the Alan he remembered. Where exactly was he and how did he end up there?

In 2006, Luke recalled that Alan had become the penultimate resident of the house, just a week before Gurdeep joined them. When prospective tenants came to look around the place, Sarah sensibly emphasised the key feature; the low rent. Alan responded by flopping his wiry frame and tangled, greasy hair onto the sofa and indicating that it would suit him just fine. All brown contours and faded shades, his own well-worn clothes camouflaged Alan perfectly against the furniture. A domestic chameleon. He seemed to fuse into the very fabric of the building. There were times, Luke swore, when Alan never made it back to his room at night, but lay there, in a state of collapse, until the first rays of morning light drove him back to the protective darkness of his bedroom. Alan may have been something of an academic sloth, but he was more helpful than the other guys with the chores, around the house. Once he found something important to get his teeth into, he would surprise everyone with a sudden burst of energy. For example, he liked cooking and often found intriguing ways to throw a few simple vegetables together and produce a worthy stir-fry or stew. No one was sure where these skills had come from. Gurdeep and Sarah joked that he would make someone a lovely partner one day. He seemed intoxicated with the praise.

Strangely, none of them ever saw him with a partner, of either sex. At times, it was as if all he really wanted to do was look after the rest of them. Although he could be frustrating at times, you couldn't dislike Alan. He seemed to really care about all of them and they noticed he had the knack of bringing out the carer in others. For example, when Sarah's sisters came down to London for her 21st birthday party, Alan was the first to offer to give up his room for the weekend. The subsequent and unexpected arrival of three of her friends prompted all three remaining male residents to do likewise, although Saul's offer to share his bed with two of the visitors was swiftly declined!

Unfortunately, Alan's energy and generosity never extended to his university work. It was all he could do to attend some of the classes. Towards the end, as failed modules piled up around him, like courtroom evidence for a prosecution, they asked him why he chose the course in the first place. He just shrugged his shoulders and laughed. 'It seemed a good idea at the time', was all he could muster.

Luke pondered these memories for several hours before deciding to make the call. He knew, deep down, that his life was far from happy, on so many different levels. Any sense of real purpose or fulfilment had eluded him, and he needed something to change.

Alan was really pleased to hear from Luke when he eventually rang. It had been many years since they had spoken to each other. Awkward platitudes punctuated the initial exchanges. Luke once again felt that sense of discomfort that surfaced when he initially read the *Facebook* message. Why make contact now, after all these years of silence, he thought Why had the message been sent to all the former house mates? Most of all, what was he inviting them to? Was he really offering some type of free holiday in a desolate mountain area, that he and Saul, guessed was somewhere between Nepal and China?

5

A woman's lament

Sarah poured another glass of *Rioja* and ambled, nonchalantly through the living room. Casting aside the intricate laced curtains, she entered the balcony area. Her mind was racing. A full moon lit up the Mediterranean skyline. In the distance, the church of St. Miguel slowly emerged, resplendent; cast in a late night, yellowish glow. Her eyes fixed upon this nocturnal beacon. The light spread, until it enveloped the outline of its ancient tower, which stood proud against the ebb and flow of an Andalusian sea.

She sat at the small table, neatly placed in front of her and gazed, again, into the night sky. Sarah was distracted for an instance, by the undignified sounds of a contented partner, inebriated with the deep slumber of sexual fulfilment. Loud nasal sounds resonating from the bedroom, confirming his tranquil bliss.

Sarah had always known that she had this gift to satisfy men in this way. They regularly came into her life, seduced by the excitement of a woman they thought sparkled with sexual chemistry. It didn't take long for her to realise that once the gyrating and coital intimacies had subsided, the real challenges would begin. How was an intelligent, modern woman, consumed with a fathomless passion to make her mark in the world, supposed to convince these partners that they should buy into her vision of life? Try to share something of it: that is, if they were realistically ever going to recognise themselves as a couple. It seemed to her that the empathy she craved, simply evaporated as soon she disrobed and began the carnal rituals. She felt used, manipulated. So why did she do it? She struggled to come up with an answer. Were men so shallow or was it just the ones that she was attracted to?

If only Brendan, lying so peacefully in the next room, could hear her anxious ponderings. If only she could find a way to penetrate his psychological defences and disclose her real self to him? In a transient moment of unfettered optimism, she indulged herself. Maybe this was a coupling that might make the stirrings of love fly and take the relationship to a whole new sphere.

Silence. Realism. *Stop pretending*, came a voice from within.

Of course, it wouldn't happen! Brendan would almost certainly fade from her life, like so many others, with protestations about the intensity of her reactions and the 'impossible' commitments being demanded from her.

She had friends who had married and started a family. However, Sarah realised that she wouldn't want to change places with any of them. She couldn't help thinking that they had settled for far less than they might have done; compromised their ambition for the security of maternal fulfilment. Marital security had come at a personal cost. On increasingly rare nights out with some of them and fuelled by the brutal honesty that too much alcohol can release, both Felicity and Ann had admitted that things had stagnated in their relationships with their respective husbands. It wasn't that they had made poor choices; it was just that the sheer monotony of domestic life had consigned much of what previously excited them, including sex, into a box, labelled 'only to be opened again, on those rare occasions, when energy levels and desire could be lifted heroically'. Never had Sarah been dragged into so much discussion about the merits of regular sleep and early nights.

The yellow haze had now fallen away from St. Miguel, as the church melted away into a darkening night shroud. Time for Sarah to rest her troubled thoughts in the comfort that sleep could offer. Sliding between the bed-sheets, she reached for her phone. She thought about the *Facebook* message that had remained unanswered and considered what to do. Yes, she would ring Alan tomorrow. After all, what was there to lose?

6

Domestic Tensions

Mohammed was running late, yet again. It wasn't, as his wife Fatima, often teased him, because there was a problem with his timekeeping. On the contrary, he believed punctuality to be a mark of respect to others. The truth was, he was simply overwhelmed by the demands of so many clients to see. He looked again at his watch and stretched a jaundiced smile across a tired face.

'Be with you in a moment, Madam. I'm so sorry you've had to wait so long.'

Mrs Howard had been waiting no more than three minutes. Sometimes he felt that *Mohammed Mohammed El Hadith* had mutated into a modern-day version of Dickens' Uriah Heap, oozing false charm with waves of empty, pungent words, as he served his master. He felt compromised in his use of such language but recognised that those in his profession needed to make their customers feel at ease, sometimes flattered, before persuading them to proverbially part with significant amounts of money. His boss, Henry, never lost the opportunity to remind Mo as he was still commonly referred to by non- Muslim friends and colleagues, of this. His lack of protest was more a statement about how he valued the lifestyle that this work now afforded.

Long gone were the days when he could afford the luxuries of such irritation. He was still resigned to accept just about any permutation of his name that wasn't directly insulting. As an intelligent Muslim, he was aware of the challenges his religion presented to others and felt it prudent to combine humour and as much patience as he could muster. After all, most of his more affluent customers were white, non-Muslims, living in a society where attitudes to Islam were now, at best cautious and sometimes even hostile. This was the legacy that he and other followers of the prophet, after whose name he bore, carried and could not escape. The impact of the wars in Iraq, Afghanistan and Syria, together with the rise and fall of the so called Islamic State, had created powerful walls of suspicion in modern Britain. A constant stream of atrocities, perpetuated by terrorists under radical Islamic banners, had led many, even moderate non-Islamic thinkers, to challenge and question those who shared a Muslim identity. Their outrage was not merely restricted to reactions to what they saw on their TV screens and smart phones.

He knew only too well that in his line of work, he had to try harder than many of his colleagues to win client confidence. His, was an environment saturated with whispered barbs and hidden judgements. Most of all, it was that look; that critical stare that conveyed unspoken judgements. A distortion riddled with injustices. This was a truth he found best to endure with quiet dignity, even if it felt like a feeble strategy to combat the absurd notion that he too, might be a terrorist sympathiser. Some of them may have been shocked to know of Muhammed's more liberal views. In truth, most of these people didn't care much what he thought. Members of his family, however, including his elderly father, were proud of what he had achieved, both in the financial sector and in his personal life. His success at work and his generosity towards the wider family had not gone un-noticed, or unappreciated by them.

So why did he feel so restless?

At 6.40pm, he climbed out of his black, metallic Jaguar and reached for his front door key. There was a moment of hesitation. A part of him was ill- prepared for one of the loving embraces that awaited behind the door. Would he be able to respond? Fatima had seen his car pulling into the drive and was waiting eagerly for him, while the children were ready to unleash their unique brand of chaotic affection. He spied their excited images through the glass pane.

'That's what children do', he thought. Those were the affections he craved for. Those were the magnetic forces that kept drawing him home. It wasn't Fatima.

'Look kids, Daddy is home', his wife bellowed down the hallway.

Mohammed opened the front door and raised a faint smile. He hugged the boys with the genuine affection of a caring father. His embrace of Fatima was less intense. He gently placed both hands on her head and lowered her forehead, before placing a solitary kiss there. She gazed into his eyes. He wondered if she could see beyond his façade; if she could shine a torch into the hidden regions of his mind? Maybe, she already had. Had Fatima discovered what lay there, yet? She embraced him nervously. Maybe, she suspected that there was a deep chasm separating and protecting her husband's thoughts from all outsiders, even her; like an old chained door that stood locked; it's key, dangling from a hook, beyond her grasp.

Had she had finally uncovered his secret?

7

Punjabi Dreams and Nightmares

Gurdeep looked at her watch again and finished her coffee. Casting an empty cereal bowl into the sink with haste, she grabbed her coat and handbag and headed for the front door. She was always keen to catch an early tube into the city. Within a couple of minutes, she was staring out at the early mists of a London dawn, from the floor of a glass elevator in her apartment block. A world in miniature unfolded to greet her sleepy eyes, as the lift descended the fourteen floors, into the street below. This was one of her favourite moments of the day. Gurdeep knew it reminded her of a previous existence; long ago in a distant land she once called home. A memory came into focus. The image was of a young girl, gazing back at her Punjabi village, as the sun began to cast aside night's blanket. She could see her as clearly as if it was only yesterday; arms, weighed heavy, with the burden of freshly pulled pails of water.

In this rustic world, the pubescent girl, like many others, was expected to rise early, each day, to perform her duties. One of these was to visit the well and bring home two large containers of water. Only then, would breakfast be taken and the journey to school begin. The sound of her footsteps provided a gentle rhythm to the growing symphony of sound generated by nature's awakening from the stillness of the night. This was an existence woven from a tapestry of vivid colours. Browns, greens and yellows merged to provide a base for dazzling plants to decorate the landscape. Bright red, gold and white flowers, provided an exquisite backdrop of pungent smells. They intoxicated her senses and kept the more unpleasant impact of excrement, decay and other foul odours at bay. There was something different about this time of the morning that had never left her, even after many years away from India.

Gurdeep indulged her memories further. Despite such pictures of contentless and beauty, there was also the spectre of darker experiences from this period that had left deep impressions on her psyche. Anxiety, tension and fear had hovered like storm clouds in the monsoon and were never far from the surface of her teenage thoughts. The images of specific family figures had followed her, like lurking shadows, into the future.

Her father, Amadeep, loomed ominously, above all of these. He stood tall, angular and strong, with fierce dark eyes that seemed to burn into her face when she caught sight of his gaze. Much of his pride and confidence stemmed from his status in the community. A *Khalsa* Sikh, baptised in the holy nectar of *Amrit*, with unflinching commitment to his faith and already an influential member of the local council, at forty- two years of age. His farming machinery business was flourishing, but there was an arrogance of certainty in the way he dismissed traditional ploughing methods in favour of his shiny new machines. What some identified and praised as confidence in future technology, others could only see as heavy- handed salesmanship. However, these voices belonged to those families whose social status did not matter in the community.

Amadeep was also flattered by the similarities sometimes made between his physical image and that of the paintings of Guru Gobind Singh, the great defender of Sikhs against persecution and creator of the *Khalsa Panth* or Sikh Nation, more than six hundred years past. Gurdeep suspected that this heightened sense of self-importance was a dangerous trait for her father to control. Despite the *Adi Granth*, or living word of God committed to sacred literature, emphasising the importance of equality of women in Sikhism, her father remained patriarchal. Instead of following the mandatory practices requiring humility and compassion, Amadeep preferred to emphasise traditional village customs and values. Women and children, especially in his household were, above all else, required to practise service and obedience. She remembered what happened when this did not occur. Her father's wrath could be terrifying. Her mother, Survinder, once burned the chapattis, after leaving them frying for too long in the oil. Amadeep had invited his brother's family around for dinner. Everyone could feel his rage towards Survinder, especially when the food was distributed. Even though no-one mentioned it, his embarrassment was plain to see. As soon as Hardeep and his family had left, Gurdeep and her brothers Banveet and Taljinder were sent to the sleeping quarter and told to read the *Guru Granith Sahib*; words and wisdom of the living God. None of them could block out the anguished cries of their mother as several blows rained down upon her. The following morning revealed the full impact of their father's anger. Their mothers face was stained with several bruises and a closed eye, which had failed to absorb the impact of one particularly savage blow. All because of some over-cooked bread, she reflected, angrily.

Her mother's demeanour, as always, spoke volumes. A silent, dignified acceptance of her husband's parochial power. It also conveyed a clear message to the children. There was no need for words or gestures. This worried the teenage Gurdeep more than anything else. She made a silent vow, in prayer that day, to Guru Nanak, the founder of the Sikh Faith. 'Oh, *Waheguru*, One God. Transform my life in obedience to your will. One day, may I demonstrate my role as both a loving partner and mother on this journey. Grant me a loving marriage, blessed with the joy of children's voices'. These words would come back to haunt her many times in the years ahead.

The tube journey took about thirty minutes, but at least the carriages usually had vacant seats at that time of the morning. Gurdeep had found the later experience, of being sandwiched between complete strangers, much more nerve- wracking than most. A mass of frenzied bodies pushing together like freshly landed fish wriggling for pockets of air, within packed boxes. She always felt overwhelmed by the smells and fragrances of humanity on the move. Like many women, she was also uncomfortable with the close- proximity of men whose attentions and involuntary touches invaded her personal space. She had walked through the nightmare that such terror could evoke in the past.

Freed from this temporary incarceration, Gurdeep stepped out onto the floor of South Kensington station and breathed deeply. The air was still crisp and inviting, as yet unsullied by the life-choking fumes of another day's pollution. A five-minute walk brought her to her place of work for the last eight years; Johnson's Chemical Enterprises. Gurdeep had what many would describe as a prestigious job, there; Development Manager for New Product Design. For someone with a Chemistry background which had recently taken her through a successful PhD route, this was a pinnacle of personal scientific achievement. However, there were few close friends in her life to celebrate it with. None of them were men. Ever since her marriage, Gurdeep had felt a painful inability to establish close relationships, particularly with adult males.

What intrigued and bewildered those close to her, was the apparent time frame involved. These marital events occurred such a long time ago, before she even started university. Over a meal at her house or sometimes at a coffee shop with Irena, a friend from *Johnson's,* she would occasionally hint that the circumstances of her wedding and subsequent events afterwards, had traumatised her so much, that she barely recognised the woman she had now become. Never again would she surrender her life to the trust of another man. The damage was irrevocable. Beyond these patchy headlines, she would not share further details to anyone. Not even to Irena. To divulge more would trigger the nightmares that needed to stay hidden: release monstrous agonies again to the surface of her mind.

Gurdeep had considered herself to have been a contented child. Maybe the submissive atmosphere at home had narrowed her expectations of freedom and personal happiness. The one exception to this was her thirst for learning. She took every opportunity to enrich her mind. Whether material was gathered from books, magazines, or even her rare experiences of watching TV; everything was analysed, processed and stored in her head. Life-changing knowledge that would fuel her ability to understand the world around her. Not for her, simply immersing her time in the skills of village craft. Nor the satisfaction displayed by others, for the tedious daily grind of domestic chores. Gurdeep, begrudgingly, completed her routines with one eye on seizing the opportunities for a different existence. This was the life her mother busied herself with, but Gurdeep, had dreamed of greater things. She tried to imagine her future and saw herself transformed by the wonders that education could bring.

Although Survinder quietly discouraged her only daughter from spending too much time in study, there was no doubting the girl's potential. She was clever. Even her father would raise a rare smile when the school reports came home. 'I know where she gets it from', he boasted, smugly. 'The education of Sikh children is very important to their parents.' This disguised a growing frustration with the more modest academic progress of his sons Banveet and Taljinder. It was their education that really concerned him. 'These boys will need to follow in my footsteps, help with the family business and one day, take over, when the time comes for me to retire', he often exclaimed, with frustration. 'They need to achieve more at school!'

His critical look towards Survinder make it clear where he felt the blame for this situation lay. 'You are too soft with them, woman.'

The boys, were, however, carrying different traits into adulthood. None of these could be blamed on their mother. Both lads had inherited their father's strong features, but not his energy and drive - they preferred to hunt snakes and climb trees to study. That was left to their little sister to engage in, during her spare time. She had also identified another, rather worrying trait: their cold indifference to the suffering of others. This had started to manifest itself in rudeness towards their mother. She put other things, like the dissection of living birds and small mammals, down to their blatant enjoyment of cruelty.

It wasn't until Gurdeep had reached the age of fifteen that she, herself became the butt of their callousness. Her transformation into a young woman, with all the physical signs of maturity, provoked a constant stream of overt and clandestine ridicule from them. There were also inappropriate touches, which sprang from their own sense of awkwardness about the female form. But of still greater concern to her, were the snippets of conversation she had started to pick up on, about prospective marriage arrangements. In her innocence, Gurdeep had assumed that such conversations lay far ahead in the future. After all she was only fifteen. Rather naively, she dreamed that it might involve someone she knew and liked. After all, her family would know that she was still coming to terms with the challenges of puberty. The monthly pains that accompanied her menstrual bleeding were a constant embarrassment to a young girl with little knowledge of her unfolding sexuality. Only her aunt, Faajal, provided the kindness and counsel she needed. Although Faajal lived in the next village, she was a regular visitor to Gurdeep's house and a big support to her younger sister, Survinder.

Gurdeep's father had been showing an increased interest in her future of late and she feared the implications. One cold October evening he summoned her and her mother to his private room at the back of their house, to tell them that Gurdeep was to be married the following year, to the eldest son of a business associate of his. Survinder's bottom lip quivered, then visibly dropped, as her eyes met her daughter's in mutual shock. She began to remonstrate meekly with her husband about her daughter's tender age, only to receive a stern rebuke.

'What? You should both be pleased with this union. He is from a good family, a suitable match and appropriate caste. This will cement our two families and secure our family status in the area'. At no point did he even look at Gurdeep, let alone ask how she felt about a wedding to a man she had never met. Gurdeep sat in silence, but her mind was racing with protestations. Her intelligence guided caution and she bowed respectfully to her father before leaving the room. However, in the security of her sleeping area, she lay awake till the early hours, staring at the myriad of stars. Only the lone howling of a wild dog reminded her that she was not completely alone, that night.

It wasn't long before she learned that her betrothed-to-be was from the neighbouring town of Sheeha, some twenty kilometres south of her village. He was also sixteen years older than her.

The wedding was set for the following Spring and on the day of the service, her local Gurdwara was filled with impressively dressed relatives and family friends, eager to witness the ceremony. Brightly wrapped gifts lay at the back of the *dirwan* or prayer hall, while others were busy preparing food in the *langar* kitchens, ready for the wedding feast. Gurdeep had finally met the groom three months earlier, when both families came together go discuss the marriage arrangements. She had not been impressed. Her intended came across as a gruff, arrogant man, not dissimilar to a younger version of her father. His clumsy attempts at dialogue left her cold and numb. There was nothing about him to suggest that tenderness and love would characterize their coupling. Instead, warning signs flashed ominously, like those that draw attention to a landslide conditions that lie ahead on a mountain road.

On the surface, everybody else seemed positive about the union and numerous aunts and cousins reinforced the blessings that the marriage would bestow on both families. Only Faajal, who had heard some unpleasant things about her niece's betrothed, hinted to her about the realities of what might lay ahead.

Several weeks before, her mother, Survinder had sat down with Gurdeep and attempted to outline the responsibilities of a wife. It sounded more like a modern-day contract for slavery.

Gurdeep was understandably more nervous than many, older brides on her wedding day. She had lead a typically innocent existence, so far; a village girl sheltered from the dangers of predatory male interest by a protective family. It hardly needed saying that she had no experience of sexual activity. All she could do was draw from the snippets of advice that had come her way from people like Faajal. Her mother, Survinder, was strangely silent on the practicalities of the subject.

She crept nervously into the marital bedroom that night, to find her new husband, Manreet, sitting on the corner of the bed, waiting eagerly for her. As Gurdeep approached he held out two hands to welcome his new wife. 'Please be gentle with me', she pleaded, nervously.

Manreet took her nimble hands and drew them closer, before kissing her on the cheek. With a sudden jerk of his right hand he pulled her onto the bed and clumsily slid his left hand down her neckline and inside her white flowered bra. Gurdeep tensed as his rough hand caressed her nipples. In an instant, his corpulent frame was bestride Gurdeep, tearing at her clothes in a frenzied act of uncontained lust. He was hurting her, but her cries of resistance were met with the back of his hand across her face. He clawed at her flesh until her under-garments had been torn away and forced himself inside her. Gurdeep winced with the pain of this aggressive invasion. His hands were all over her fragile body, biting and scratching. Tears fell from Gurdeep's crimson eyes as she was engulfed in a savage attack. Even in her innocence, she knew this was not love.

Bruised and violated, Gurdeep was finally able to slink across to the far side of the bed, as Manreet slumbered, intoxicated with the insanity of sexual violence. This was only the beginning of her ordeal. Similar nights would follow.

Survinder visited her daughter regularly at her new home, but turned her head away, when confronted with the sight of Gurdeep's bruises and her obvious sense of desperation. 'Is this what men understand by love?', she whispered to her mother.

The older victim of abuse sat next to her, without speaking. Survinder eventually hugged her daughter and started to weep. What her mother couldn't see in this embrace was the defiance written across Gurdeep's tortured face. Her dreams of marriage may have been fractured, but she was not going to sink into oblivion and despair, accepting such outrage lightly.

Eight weeks later, while Manreet was away on a business trip in Amritsar, Gurdeep packed a small bag. Inside, there was a change of sari, other clothing and some personal toiletries. It also contained a significant sum of rupees, converted from dowry gifts and the sale of some small jewellery pieces. She was careful not to arouse suspicion by trading in items at her local village market.

She had confided to her aunt, Faajal, about her living nightmare. She had had to talk to someone. Faajal was not surprised. After much deliberation and soul-searching, a plan of release began to take shape in Gurdeep's head. She must leave him. She didn't know where she would go or how she would get there. All she knew was that each despairing day she stayed was bringing her a step closer to insanity and self-destruction.

Faajal took some convincing, when her niece found the courage to share her intentions with her. Although her aunt was sympathetic, her empathy was wrapped in warnings about the dangers her plan carried. Eventually, Faajal realised this young woman was not going to be dissuaded. She was adamant. All Faajal could do was to try to assist her, by removing some of the initial obstacles. Make her plan more likely to succeed. She implored upon her that there was no going back. The risks were immense. She provided Gurdeep with additional money, to help her escape. This would be at some risk to her own safety, if discovered. The consequences didn't bear thinking about, if the truth was ever to emerge. Gurdeep, meanwhile, waited patiently for her chance and Manreet's trip provided the perfect opportunity.

The sun beamed invitingly through cracks in the back door, as she walked away from everything she knew and had once loved. The risk of being discovered made her shiver. Taking the smaller paths through the wheat fields, evading the neighbouring farms to avoid detection, she took a chance on the main road and flagged down a dilapidated grey truck that was moving slowly towards her. The driver, an older man in his sixties with a long greyish-white beard and green, patterned turban, looked surprised at the sight of the young woman petitioning for a lift.

'Where are you going daughter?', he said. 'These roads are not always safe for lone female travellers.'

'Please, sir. I need to get to Pandeer to catch a train. Will you help me?'

The man gazed compassionately at her. He looked deeply into her eyes and felt her anxiety. He himself, was the father of two daughters. He realised that the look of misery on this prematurely -aged face was a cry for help. 'Get in, daughter.'

Thirty minutes later, he dropped her at the roadside, close to the train station.

'Whatever troubles you, young lady, may God keep you safe.'

'Thank you, sir', the teenage bride replied.

In that moment, her childhood prayer to Guru Nanak resonated in her head. 'Some men are capable of kindness', she mused.

Once out of the Punjab, she felt a little safer. Just another face amongst thousands of faceless others. However, this was still a new world of uncertainties and dangers for a Punjabi village girl with little experience of the wider world. Sipping from a small cup of sweet *chai*, while staring at the sun as it set vividly behind the mountain range before her, she knew there was no turning back. A guarded smile broke through her defences. Gurdeep couldn't recall the last time that had happened.

Back at her home, a hornet's nest was forming with terrible implications. Her absence had finally been discovered in the late afternoon and accusations flew like deadly arrows. Faajal remained silent about her missing niece and pleaded ignorance. Her mother, assumed to be complicit in this 'shameful' act, was enduring another savage beating. Manreet was questioning the character of the family he had married into and her father and sons, burning with shame and rage, would have torn Gurdeep limb from limb, if they had found her and suspected that she intended never to return.

8

An unusual business

Alan was feeling more than a little tense. Was it the tightness of a new shirt collar, further tautened by the smart blue neck- tie holding it together? He reached, awkwardly, for the muscle at the back of his neck. These days, he wasn't used to such constricted clothing. The humid atmosphere in the room didn't help, either. A dilapidated air-conditioning unit on the wall, was failing spectacularly, to offer any relief. Opening his top button, he was distracted by a curious thought. He visualised himself, standing at the gallows. Was this how the first moments of being hanged felt like? He imagined the full weight of his body crashing down, breaking his neck and snapping his spinal column. He watched himself, rendered motionless, as the life force drifted from his body.

Amit Shakya, his friend, sat next to him, attempting to mask his own nervousness, by clicking his fingers, sporadically. As if conscious of Alan's anxiety, He pinched his companion's arm. 'Are you ok Alan?', he whispered.

'Fine, my friend. It's just a little humid in here for me.'

They were interrupted by approaching footsteps.

'Mr Rogers. Mr Shakya. We're ready for you now.' Alan's mind quickly re-focused. A smart, well- groomed gentleman, with a waxed moustache and furrowed brow, was leaning over him. Alan looked up and wondered how many others have sat where he was sitting. He wasn't just referring to his choice of seat. He felt he was trapped within a cauldron, ready to melt. 'I'm Udgam Vogal, regional manager for Property Purchases, National Parks. Pleased to meet you, gentlemen.'

Alan and Amit exchanged limp handshakes and followed their avuncular escort, into the large room on the left.

The atmosphere more resembled that of a court-room than a regional government office. In front of them sat a small woman with tight, permed grey hair, dressed in a dark, blue sari. Her eyes were cast downwards, as if in prayer, towards the semi-circular, oak desk that separated the panel from them. Next to her, was a stout gentleman in a pin-striped suit with a pink carnation in his lapel. He smiled benignly. Alan took his seat and bid them good morning.

Simultaneously, Amit bowed respectably and offered a dignified *Namaste,* before sitting down next to his English friend.

The last member of the panel was a younger woman, possibly in her mid-thirties, with long brown hair, who viewed them inquisitively. Mr Vogal took his seat at the end of the row and started to introduce Mr Sharma and the other members of the panel. Each nodded in recognition of their name and role within the administration. Alan tried to look interested, but inside, he was only concerned about one thing: Would his request, be successful or not? For ten minutes, he nodded his head as he listened to each of the officials. They took great pains to outline their initial reaction to Alan's proposal, which lay in front of them. Alan was still no wiser about the outcome.

'This is an unusual application, gentlemen and that is why I've asked some of my colleagues to consider it with me', Mr Vogal continued. 'As I'm sure you are both aware, the Nepalese Government does not allow foreigners to purchase land or property in this country. Nor, may non-citizens be gifted or acquire land, especially in a National Park area like the *Annapurna.* You may have heard rumours about the civil code changing to allow westerners to buy flats in Kathmandu, but I assure you these are only rumours. And it certainly won't affect the restrictions on national park property. I assume that is why your name is on the contract of purchase, Mr Shakya. I understand that you are from the district of Pinang and have lived there all your life.'

Amit nodded.

Mr Vogal continued glancing down at the sheet of paper in front of him. 'A farmer, with a small homestead, I believe.' He scrutinised the details before him and continued. 'You're a man of modest means...' He peered over his spectacles towards Amit.

'Yes, sir', Amit replied.

'But according to this paperwork, you have acquired sufficient funds to buy this large property, further up the valley. And that money has come from the gentleman sat next to you, has it not?'

Amit continued to nod.

Mr Vogal turned towards Alan. 'What I don't understand, Mr Rogers, is why you are pouring so much capital into a property you will not own. There is nothing to stop Mr Shakya from ejecting you from the place as soon as he takes possession of the property deeds. It is, indeed, a laudable plan to employ several local people at the house, but the risk of you losing everything is huge, is it not, sir?'

Alan took a deep breath and scanned the faces of the panel for evidence of some reaction to his statement. He stood up to address the panel. 'Sir/Ladies. I hear your words and understand your concerns. This majestic country of yours has given me so much in my short stays among you. Now, I would like to give something back. In no other place, have I encountered such raw, awe -inspiring beauty and such human resilience to the elements. It changes people. It has certainly changed me. I realise that many indigenous people here, are poor. Especially in the remote mountains. They may sometimes cast envious glances towards Kathmandu, or towards the western world, with all its wealth and power. But we know that human fulfilment and happiness, lies along a different path. I want to set up my own, humble legacy, for local people. People like Amit, here, so that they can preserve their values and culture in the high mountains. To that end, the farmhouse he seeks to purchase, will be a sanctuary. But I will be no more than a guest, oiling the wheels, with the necessary finance to maintain the centre. As you know, my visa restrictions will prevent me from being there all the time. But I know this *sanctuary* will be in good hands, when I am away. It will also be an opportunity for some of the refugees from the government village, nearby, to gain employment there.'

Mr Vogal cleared his throat and addressed Alan. 'We would like to ask you a question, Mr Rogers. What exactly, are Mr Shakya and your band of workers intending to do with the farm, if he does become the new owner?'

Alan un-hunched his shoulders and responded. 'Although I have only been in the country a short time, I've come to recognise the uniqueness of this place. Many visitors come from Europe and beyond. They walk the sacred paths of Nepal and return home. The difference for me, is that I want to stay. Eventually, I want to gain Nepalese citizenship, although I realise that this will take time. I do recognise the need for development and support among poor families in the mountains and want to use what money I have acquired, to make my own small impact. In short, to turn this isolated out-post of Himalayan beauty into a refuge for reflection and understanding. A place where people can come to find rest and inspiration. Just as I have done. I believe I can provide work for half a dozen local people, looking after the guests whom I hope to attract. But most of all, this will be my spiritual home. A place between the mountains, where people can bring troubled minds and maybe find a little peace. My great hope is that you will support us, in the project.'

Amit finally found his voice. 'Good morning everyone. I would like to say something, please, if I may. Yes, I am a poor mountain farmer from the region of Pinang. Like my neighbours, life has been a struggle, supporting my family and trying to carve out an existence in the foothills of the *Himalaya*. I used to watch the foreigners walking past my farm, with their brightly coloured jackets and expensive boots, intrigued by their determination and resilience. I felt I had nothing to offer these outsiders. But their desire for local people to escort them through the more dangerous high passes and glaciers, has enabled me to find additional work as a guide. A few have also stayed the occasional night at my house. I've been surprised how interested many of them are in Nepalese culture. Meeting these westerners has challenged me about my life, too. I have learned that even a simple farmer has something to offer. Most westerners come to enjoy the scenery and then go home with their memories and photographs, never to return. Alan is not like them. As soon as he leaves, he is busy planning for his next visit. Why is this? Only because he cares about us. He wants to leave something here, maybe, in a small way, like the great Edmund Hilary did in the past, with his school programmes.

'In this valley there are many people like me. Trying to scratch out an existence in a hostile terrain. When men are unemployed, they sometimes turn to other things to fill their time. You know what I mean. We find them unconscious on village dirt tracks, drunk, or disorientated by over-indulgence in cannabis and other drugs. Sometimes they fight and seriously hurt each other. Local rice wine and drugs, not western trekkers, are destroying our communities. Alan's money will not just buy a property. It will provide jobs, hope. There will be work for local people. Mountain guides, cooks, cleaners, teachers will all be required.

'Few people are like Alan. His generosity and kindness are truly humbling. His spirit is at home here. He has a 'Nepalese' soul. I think we should all support him in this. As for our friendship, he knows the respect, I and my family and friends, hold for him. Where such a bond exists, there is no room for deception or betrayal. We have come to trust him, and he trusts us. He knows that'.

Mr Vogal looked across at Alan, inquisitively and exclaimed:

'What you and Mr Shakya have said is laudable, sir, and you are not the first foreigner to be inspired by such altruistic motives. But you have chosen an isolated and dangerous place to do this. It can be extremely cold in the Winter; the snows sometimes cut these communities off from the outside world for several months. Avalanches, floods and poor growing conditions all add to the dangers and challenges of living in such a place. Would it not be more sensible seeking somewhere closer to Pokhara or even Kathmandu?'

Alan looked confidently at each member of the panel in turn and said 'Yes, of course, the safety net in these places is small, more precarious than other parts of the country, where help can be stronger and nearer when problems arise. But part of the importance of what I want to do is connected to the vulnerability of living away from these comforts. Being exposed to the forces of nature can also galvanize one's spirit to meet such challenges with courage and humility. If Hinduism and Buddhism teaches us anything about the human condition, it is surely that we need to connect to the land and embrace the challenge to find our inner selves, to seek the spiritual, through loving-kindness and humility.'

Mr Vogal looked at him, and nodded, approvingly. He asked Alan and Amit to leave the room for a few minutes, while the committee members deliberated over their decision. Ten minutes later, they were called back.

The chairman of the panel reminded everyone that there hadn't been any other offers for the property. The owner, he pointed out, had moved away, last year, to Pokhara. 'He has put the place up for sale, asking what many considered to be an exorbitantly expensive price for the farm. No-one around there had shown interest in purchasing the place. They could hardly afford it. And why would they? The soil there is poor, and it is uncomfortably close to dangerous mountains with all the threats they pose.' Mr Vogal stood to announce that they would support Alan's application. Even Mrs Bagara raised her chin a little, to break into a nervous smile.

The lady with the long dark hair, Miss Arturanba, seemed most pleased with the decision and added that she was looking forward to hearing how the project would develop. Mr Sharma raised his copious frame and informed Amit that a copy of the full contract would be with him within the next couple of days. Alan took another pull at the knot in his tie and breathed a sigh of relief. Months of planning had gone into this enterprise and he wasn't sure what he was going to do if the office had said 'No'. There was no plan 'B'. As he walked out of the room, discarding the offending tie into a bin close by, he felt excited for the first time in years. He hugged Amit. There would be a place between the Mountains, after all. His dream was about to take shape.

9

African diamonds

Alan had been living in Nepal, at least part of the time, for almost three years. It was costing him a fortune in visa fees. Like many westerners, he was initially drawn by the majesty of the hills and he ended up trekking many of her high mountain trails. His previous seven years had read like a transformational rollercoaster of good fortune.

Having left university without a degree and little idea of what to do next, he soon grew tired of months spent in menial employment, barely earning the minimum wage. Eventually, living back with his less than impressed parents, he realised that his life was heading into meltdown. What could he do? Having always enjoyed playing around with numbers and spread-sheets and with renewed energy, (the source of which quietly baffled him), he decided to study accountancy, at college, for two nights a week. To his surprise, he quite enjoyed it. Within three years, he was working at a local firm in the payments office. His grasp of figures and data made the transition to this new venture successful. Even his parents were puzzled. Although they never came out and said it, it was clear that they had just about given up on Alan.

Unfortunately, having secured a full- time post and with money now coming in to his normally empty bank account, Alan became restless again. His gaze drifted across the London skyline and out towards further horizons. Africa, the 'dark continent,' as his old geography books referred to it, always intrigued him. All those stories of mysterious tribes and exotic animals re-surfaced from his boyhood dreams. What an adventure it might be to live there for a while, he thought! In fact, to live anywhere that wasn't London would be exciting. In the evenings, he buried himself in the small job ads that littered the internet. Eventually, one vacancy aroused his curiosity: *English- speaking accountant required, familiar with the demands of maintaining the financial affairs of a small, British owned business: location: South Africa.*

Further on, he noted something else about the position that appealed to him: *Accommodation on site available to a single person.* Alan had been a single person all his life, even though he wasn't quite sure why. Maybe, he wasn't meant to get that close to people.

The telephone interview confirmed the company's desire to appoint an English national and he, it seemed, turned out to be the only candidate who fell into that category. Six weeks later, he was on a British Airways flight to Johannesburg. He had never been any further than Southern Spain in his life.

Arriving in South Africa to start a new job with a jewellery firm, his status quickly rose, largely due to the unlikely friendship he developed with the company boss, Jacob Martin. Although there was twenty years difference in age between the men, Jacob recognised something in Alan that few had seen before. Potential. Beneath the façade of an easy- going, reflective dreamer, lay someone with real substance. A man, who with a little encouragement and direction, could achieve much more. Someone, who could sense what might need to happen next, in this small jewellery business, owned by an ex-pat on the northern suburbs of Johannesburg.

With Alan taking up residence in the separate flat at the back of Jacob's house, they gradually began to spend more time together, socially. The barriers that often characterise an employer employee relationship faded away, with Jacob treating the young Englishman more like a son. The older man had spent much of his early life travelling around different parts of the African continent and in Asia, on business. Alan enjoyed hearing his stories, often lubricated with generous supplies of Cape wine or local beer from his host's cellar. Not only had he become a key participant in his boss's life, but he was providing Jacob with the companionship he no longer enjoyed, since the tragic death of his wife Rebecca in a car accident, three years earlier.

After a couple of contented years, working diligently and doing his best to immerse himself in South African culture, something happened that would transform Alan's life. It certainly wasn't engineered by one of those humungous ideas he used to speak about in his student days. The things that were going to astound everyone, like 'sandstorms in the desert'. This was more about the hand of fate shining gloriously and benignly, upon him, when he least expected it.

Jacob had received some information, from a close business contact, about a new diamond speculation on the edge of Southern Botswana, not far from the South African border. Although it lay, geographically close to the world- famous Debswana mine, which was partially owned by the government, this plot of land had not been explored or mined for rare stones. The associate was brimming with confidence, when he spoke to Jacob. 'Might be worth investing a few *rand* in this one. It's going to be big, my friend!'

Jacob decided to buy significant shares in the company which had staked its claim on the land, after his old business friend had advised him that there could be 'serious' money to be made there. Like a guardian protecting his young protégé, the avuncular owner had asked Alan if he would like to divert a small part of his wages towards the venture. He needed to know quickly. This was not problematic for a young man with few needs and even fewer drains on his salary. He was a willing participant and thanked Jacob for the tip. 'Who knows', he thought,' it should make more than the bank's interest rates'

What unfolded next was stunning. Three months later, the company unearthed a huge seam of precious stones; much larger than anyone had dared hope for. The nearby town of Jwaneng started to live up to its etymological meaning. The local paper carried a translated media boast that it was the hidden place of small, valuable stones. It didn't realise what was also there. It clearly didn't know about the larger precious rocks that lay hidden and un-touched beneath the surface. So valuable, in fact, were the diamonds they dug from the seam, that the company shares just 'went through the roof'.

Jacob's 'insider friend' did his best to wriggle out of his commitment to share this good fortune with him, but Jacob had already purchased and registered his documents. This included a significant portfolio in Alan's name, too. Within six months these were changing hands for enormous fees and Alan, unexpectedly, and for the first time in his life, found himself quite wealthy.

His financial situation improved still further, when Jacob, a widower without children, had a massive heart attack six weeks later and died, leaving Alan a significant financial legacy. The shock and worry of suddenly acquiring too much wealth turned out to be more dangerous to his health than the usual anxieties about paying the bills. Largely out of respect for his deceased benefactor, he stayed on at the firm for a while, but there was a sadness in his heart. Jacob had been like another father to him and he missed his charismatic presence in his life. Furthermore, the atmosphere in the company soon changed after the funeral. Jacob's two, senior colleagues Neil and Richard, resented their bosses' generosity to Alan and made their feelings only too clear, even though they too, had benefitted, generously, from the will. They were keen to continue running the company but not with Alan on board. He realised that it would be best to move on, but to what and where? Having sampled the excitement of Africa, he was hardly ready to return home to Britain.

Later that week, at his local bar, the Mombasa Lodge, he got chatting to a business man from India. This stocky visitor, in his forties, dressed in a crisp grey suit, with black, oily hair combed back across his forehead, introduced himself from the adjacent bar stool. Aarva was a retail buyer for a chain of cut-price clothes shops in Delhi. What began as a casual exchange of pleasantries, developed into a conversation about memorable moments and places they had visited. It was clear that Aarva had travelled extensively and Alan, once again, feasted on the tales and sights, described by his drinking companion. His own offering of London and Torremolinos, in Southern Spain, were much more modest examples, by comparison. Given Aarva's background, and especially some of the challenges he shared about his low- caste status, from the 'Shudra' servant or tenant farmer caste, it intrigued Alan to hear that the location that stood out among others for him, was not one of the iconic capitals of the East or any of Europe's hedonistic playgrounds, but a town in Eastern Nepal; Pokhara. This second city of Nepal, lay to the east of it's much larger and more illustrious capital, Kathmandu.

Alan had never heard of Pokhara. The only thing he knew about Nepal was that some of the men from there had a special regiment in the British Army: the Gurkha's. They were reputed to be incredibly strong: something to do with growing up in the thin mountain air. Even this snippet was gleamed from another source; his dad and mum who frequented the local Gurkha restaurant in South London.

It wasn't completely true that he knew next to nothing about Nepal. When he was a child, Alan had enjoyed lacing his boots and walking local hills in the UK. His parents had ignited this interest in him at an early age, with regular trips to North Wales and Devon. He remembered being enthralled by a television programme about Mount Everest and the Himalayan range of mountains that surrounded it.

Unfortunately, something had happened at that time that cast a dark spectre across much of his later childhood: the death of his younger brother Neil. It was whilst out on such a walk, in the lower hills around Bets-y-Coed, in Snowdonia, that Neil was taken ill. At first everyone thought it was just a touch of fatigue. On the way back, within sight of the car, he fainted. The subsequent trip to the hospital in Bangor that night, sent alarm bells ringing and began a chain of events that would end in tragedy.

Neil's loss of consciousness, a weakened heart beat and inability to swallow, led his anxious family into a waking nightmare. A rare form of cancer had consumed his young life within months, leaving his family bereaved and desperate. Neil was only ten years old when he died. His brother was barely two years older.

Allan's old walking boots still lay in the shoe cupboard, gathering dust, alongside those of his distraught parents. They hadn't been used since.

The first hour merged into a second at the Mombasa Bar, as Alan became increasingly fascinated by Aarva's interest in Pokhara and the surrounding mountain areas. His companion went on to describe a huge lake lying at the end

40

of the town, with tranquil views of the Annapurna skyline. There was a central area packed with small shops and cafés, catering for the trekkers who had come down from the mountains. He learned that a circular walking route, around the central massifs of the Annapurna range, brought visitors to a richly varied landscape, pitted with small villages, rich in ethnically diverse communities.

'To trek the entire length of the Annapurna massif would take nearly three weeks and involve the completion of over 220 kilometres', explained Aava. 'I have only walked a small section of the route. but others described where it could be accessed. Heading east from Pokhara, most people would start this undertaking on the edge of what they call the Pokhara Khundi route, at Besi Shamar. A gravel road meanders through this part of the route, (known as the Jeepable road) staying close to the Marsyangdi Nadi river. It eventually comes to a halt. Beyond there, only an ambitious motor bike, or traditional horse- driven carts and pack animals, enable goods to be transported to the more isolated villages'.

Although some of these details sailed through Alan's head and out, again, he was genuinely enthralled by what he heard. 'And beyond there? enquired Alan?

'Beyond there…' Aava continued, '…Small rural farming communities dotted around the base of the mountains.' Life unfolds pretty much as it has always done. With the possible exception of mobile -phones!' He smiled. 'Even the most impoverished residents seem to have one these, nowadays'.

'How do you know all this?' the Englishman blurted out.

'When I am not buying clothing, I like to put on my boots and head towards the high peaks. I feel so much more alive in these places. Somehow, closer to my inner self, my *atman* or soul. I met many walkers from around the world, who told me about these hidden valleys and the people who live there. My family, back home, think I am a little strange, but you Europeans like to climb mountains. Yes?'

Alan thought about the old walking boots, hidden away in a dark corner of a cupboard at his parent's home. 'Err. I guess so,' his companion replied. 'At least some do.' He closed his eyes and tried to imagine the ambitious and mind-tingling reality of living in such a place, cut off from the outside world for five months of the year by landslides and heavy snowfall. As Aarva rose to make his farewells, Alan was already thinking about his next destination.

Over the next few weeks, he spent much of his spare time and evenings, researching the Annapurna district of Nepal. He even invested in a new pair of walking boots. It felt strange, after all this time, tying the thick laces around metal studs at the front of his new footwear. Staring out at the hills in the far distance, this man was once again a child, about to embark upon an unknown journey that was full of exciting possibilities. Although the immediate area where he lived was quite flat and heavily populated, a short, fifteen- minute car ride took him to the edge of an outcrop of granite hills. Although dark and foreboding, they seemed, he felt, to be calling out to him. He thought again on what Aarva had said about feeling 'more alive' in these elevated landscapes. Although he was sure that Africa was very different to Nepal, as he walked, he wondered about the attraction of its peacefulness; it's solitude and remoteness. Maybe, despite the physical environment, it was safer than the crime ridden cities of South Africa and similar sprawling, urban centres in other countries.

In one sense, Alan had always felt alone. It wasn't that he didn't enjoy the company of others. He did. It was just that he didn't seem to rely on people, like so many that he knew. The only exception to this had been his experience of living with his flatmates in Ealing, all those years ago. He remembered feeling happy then, although he wasn't sure why. Did he have much in common with Mohammed, Saul, Sarah, Luke, or Gurdeep? Maybe not, if he was honest. Luke had been a closer friend, but he hadn't seen him for several years now. And yet?

An idea began to take shape and crystallised in his head, like the beckoning image of an old friend, standing at the door. What if he could assemble these former flatmates for some sort of re-union? Bring them together after all these years. But for what purpose? In his eyes, a clarity started to emerge. There could be but one purpose to this venture. To try to help them. To support them in their lives. He began thinking about their individual personalities and the challenges they faced as young adults. Would they have changed much in the decade that had passed? It would be fascinating to find out.

With all this money now at his disposal, he resolved to find out where they were and do something positive for them. But what, exactly?

10

Amit

Alan had made his first visit to the Marsyangdi Nadi river valley, two years previously. As he arrived in late August, the long, hot, summer days were starting to retreat, as azure skies welcomed the cooler afternoons. Plummeting blasts of cold, late night air chilled the landscape. The advent of Winter was close. November, he had been told, was usually such a good month for trekking in Nepal. With its warm rays of sunshine still baking the morning hours, it invited the unsuspecting traveller to tread its paths.

He found accommodation without too much trouble, at local trekking huts that had been built around the edges of Dharapani and Chame. As he continued to follow the course of the river, the terrain became wilder and more desolate. The high peaks of 'Annapurna Two and Four', leaned menacingly down towards the tracks that meandered through the network of isolated homesteads and farms.

For a moment, he almost forgot he was travelling alone. Surprisingly, he didn't feel perturbed or frightened. What lay around him, both bewildered and bewitched this curious outsider. There were still plenty of trekkers on the paths to bump into and sometimes exchange stories with, over a drink or meal. Occasionally, he would meet those who spoke English and he was able to indulge himself in more extensive discussions. He wasn't the only one travelling solo.

Towards the end of his third week there, his walk one day, took him to the outskirts of some particularly dramatic scenery. The wind had picked up and his journey had sapped the energy from his bones. He needed to take a break. Alan came to an old dilapidated lodge, built, overlooking a deep ravine. He decided to stop. A good place for the night, or so he thought. The sympathetic proprietor told him what he didn't want to hear. His four guest bunks had already been booked for that night. He shrugged his tired shoulders, nonchalantly, and moved on, but the same exchange of words was repeated at the next lodge. He was starting to feel concerned. Surely, there were always places to stay out here?

As he approached the third lodge, he was almost in panic mode. The cheery restaurant owner broke the bad news. His impending meltdown mellowed a little by the offer of a tent at the back of the building. At least it was somewhere.

'I have thick, yak-hair sleeping bags. They keep you warm, Mister. Very cheap price!', the eager householder declared.

His attention was distracted by excited German voices, as they arrived back from their day's walk. One of them was taking HIS bed! Alan took a sip of hot ginger tea and sat down to rest his aching knees.

From the corner of the seated area, a wiry looking man, probably in his late thirties, sat, eating a plate of lentils and rice. What caught Alan's attention, was that the man seemed to have been listening to his conversation with the lodge owner.

'Excuse me for interrupting, Sir,' he eventually said. 'I am a local farmer and mountain guide in this district. I overheard your discussion about a bed for the night. If you are interested, I have a room at my house. Just outside the village. It is a modest dwelling, but you would be welcome to stay with my family. It will be warmer than the tent.'

Alan was not as naïve as he sometimes looked. He knew that there were risks in accepting such offers from a stranger. Should he act on his instinct? The man seemed genuine. The lodge owner eased his fears by suddenly offering a positive character reference, on behalf of the farmer.

'He's an honest man, my friend. I 've known his family for years. Although it will cost me a few lost rupees, I must admit it, it would be a wiser option. It's going to be cold tonight. But you must promise to come back and eat at my restaurant, tomorrow. Best food around here,' he boasted. The stranger nodded. Alan's gut reaction had been confirmed. He decided to accept the offer.

That was how he met Amit. Later that night, as the wind, howled and snow flurries danced around, outside Amit's house, he realised he'd made the right choice.

In the morning, the snow had disappeared, and the sun had brought warmth to the landscape. Amit enquired about Alan's itinerary for the day. He wanted to see a local glacier and was happy for his host to accompany him, as a guide. Alan thought the suggested price, including his overnight stay, was derisory! Amit's wife, Anwa, was an enthusiastic host. While her two young children satisfied their curiosity about him, with tentative touches of Alan's hand and blonde, straggly hair, she busied herself, introducing the Englishman to her humble offerings of local food. As they set off, fortified by delicious home-made soup and bread, neither man fully realised that a monumental friendship was in the process of being formed.

As they walked, it became clear to Alan, that there was more to Amit than he had initially realised. This self-evidently poor, rural, mountain farmer, was also the custodian of a vast reservoir of endless, fascinating facts and knowledge about the region. He was only too pleased to share them with his visitor.   As they approached the glacier, the sun bathed the distorted ice pack, with glorious colours, highlighting the myriad of strange objects trapped beneath its surface. Amit told the story of an unknown man, whose frozen corpse tumbled from the glacier, two years before. 'These glaciers are like, how do you say, time trap's, he continued. 'Like a monstrous beast, they suck you in; devour you, and leave you there for many years, to travel with the movement of the ice, wherever it flows. Then, when the monster has grown tired of its plaything, he spits it out again. As the sun melts, a hole appears at the end of the ice flow, to release its prey. Normally, it's rock, stones or pieces of wood. But sometimes, we find an animal, like a goat, or even a lost trekker!' The mountain farmer broke into a loud laugh. 'But not today, my friend. I will keep the monster at bay'.

Alan grinned.

Returning to his story, Amit explained that the body had been examined by a medical team and thought to be more than a hundred and fifty years old. They could still see signs of what he had swallowed, that fatal day of his demise. 'At least he'd eaten well,' Amit joked. 'People vanish up here, all the time', he said. 'Only last year, a couple from Italy went missing, after trekking without a guide, in the Chulu Glacier, east of here. They may end up disgorged from one of the glaciers, one day or, more likely, be forever entombed in the snow and ice'. He paused, and his face became sterner. 'This is the Annapurna and it is every bit as dangerous as the Kumbu Glacier, at Everest.'

They climbed to the top of the ice wall and looked across to the mountains behind. 'Be careful with this section', Amit implored him. 'The ice up here, is thin. I don't want to have to dangle a rope down there, to pull you out!'

Alan needed no reminders about caution. He remained focused, but in a state of controlled exhilaration. He could hear his heart pumping, with each precarious step. Neither the rising wind, nor the dropping temperatures, could mask his mood. He was having the time of his life.

It wasn't until two days later that Alan returned to the 'Hidden Falls' guesthouse to fulfil his promise. The owner was particularly pleased. Alan had brought extra mouths to feed, having insisted that Amit's wife, Anwa, and their two children, accompany them.

Alan returned several times to the Annapurna National Park, in the following three years. He always found time to visit Amit. They talked for hours about the contrasting worlds they lived in. His days in Amit's farm, brought home to him vividly, what a daily battle for survival his family faced. Farming could only provide a basic subsistence. Finding trekkers to guide through the unchartered areas was vital to bring additional money in.

Slowly, it dawned upon Alan that his desire to live and work in Nepal, and Amit's challenges, in looking after his loved ones, could be linked. A eureka moment came to him. He would use his money for something unique. Something that could help his friend and assist him in realising a growing dream. If he could find a way to purchase a larger building and invite paying guests to stay, then there would be seasonal work for Amit and other people from the area.

Amit was humbled by his friend's generosity but warned that such a venture was not without its problems. Not least of these being, that only Nepalese citizens could buy property in the country. Alan's mind was on over-drive. The germ of an idea had crept into his head. He resolved to start looking for a place immediately.

11

Regrets

Saul picked up the photo that had slipped, tantalisingly, from a pile of faded magazines. It landed on the floor in front of him. The odour of stale dust made his nose twitch. He brushed away this extra coating of colour and stared at the picture, carefully, for several seconds, like someone greeting the unexpected arrival of a post-card from exotic shores. Five youthful faces stared back at him from a once familiar section of Brighton beach. To the right of the fifth figure, whom he instantly recognised as a slimmer version of his friend, Luke, stood the familiar pillars of this town's famous pier. To the left, next to his own image, was a tall, attractive female. Her copious locks of black hair seemed to be swaying in harmony, with a gusty sea breeze. She looked happy. Eventually, a name surfaced from his clouded memory.

'Martha, or was it Maureen?', he mused, as he attempted to identify the face. 'I wonder what became of her?', he pondered, awkwardly, with a tinge of superficial regret. He recalled her smile, melting into tears of disappointment when he abandoned her. These moments were not rare events in the life of Saul. The last ten years had been littered with the images of what had now become a legion of exes; many cast aside, with no possibility of playing any part in his future. Their names had been consigned to a place far beyond where most of his friends locked their intimate experiences from the past. It was how he coped with the impact of disappointment.

Saul now found himself looking at other faces which seemed to rise from a pile of scattered magazine covers on the floor. His old 'porn' mags! Why hadn't he thrown them away? He started to thumb his way through some of them. Mawkish contours of female seduction leaped towards him. Pouting lips, twisted with lewd, inviting curves, exposing their genitalia in postures of vulgar, frenzied licentiousness. It was as if these images had mobilised a wave of anger. It was targeted, in that moment, entirely upon him. Deep down, he knew that none of this material was authentic or pure. It wasn't even erotic! It simply pandered to the sexual inadequacies of the weak and indulgent. People like himself. He realised that part of him, was still that awkward fourteen- year- old adolescent, gawking at those rude bits that used to make him and his friends snigger. How many boys kept their teenage pornography mags for so long? Saul felt a little embarrassed. He had suspected for some time now, that his objectification of women would come at a price. He had struggled to develop any of his romantic relationships into something long-term. Why was that, he wondered? Despite an undoubted charm and physical attractiveness, the females he now encountered in his life were increasingly wary of him. Had he become that transparent? So superficial? Why had he purchased so much of this 'literature' in the past? Even the few friends he could count upon, were mostly in regular relationships, now, and at least attempting to learn how to share their lives and not just their desires, with a partner who loved them.

Although he told others that his domestic situation, living by himself, was a personal choice, the truth was more painful to digest. He was still, at heart, that excitable teenager who regularly wanted to satisfy his lustful urges with the smells and touches of a new female. He still wanted to boast to his mates, people like Luke, about his ability to deceive and compromise the decency of so many girls who had, in the past, became snarled in his seductive net. For a few seconds, Saul felt the embers of an emotion he rarely recognised or understood. Shame.

12

Re-union at the City Arms

Saul and Luke had arranged to meet at a local pub, straight after work, on Tuesday evening. They wanted to discuss further, their separate telephone conversations with Alan. Both men harboured initial concerns about the invitation. They wondered about his sanity and shared these worries with open candour.

'Do you think he's lost his 'marbles' out there?', Saul questioned his friend, as he finished his first pint of lager.

'You have to ask questions about how he came to end up in such a place'

'If you ask me, he's looking for something from us. Something to help him justify what he's doing with his life in Nepal'

Luke nodded repeatedly, in the way he often did, when Saul held the floor. 'The thing I don't get, Saul, is that he's willing to splash out almost eight hundred pounds each on the air fares alone. Why would anybody want to do that, after all this time?'

'And for people he doesn't really know anymore', Saul added. 'I'm sure we've all changed quite a lot over the years.'

'What do you think he's hoping to gain from us, if we decide to accept the invitation?'

Saul announced he was off to the bar for more drinks.

'I'll have pint of Stella this time.'

As they consumed their drinks, they agreed that it had been sensible to try and contact their other three ex-flatmates, to see what they thought about Alan's offer. Saul had tracked down Sarah and Gurdeep, through their *Facebook* pages and Mohammed had found Saul through the same source. Then, although it was rather short notice, Saul had messaged the other three, inviting them to the 'City Arms', slightly later because he really wanted to clarify his own position on this with Luke before speaking to the others.

Mohammed had indicated that he didn't think he wanted to participate in the venture. Gurdeep was also rather dismissive. The only one who confirmed she would turn up, that evening, was Sarah.

Saul picked up his i-Phone and opened his *Facebook* account to share Mohammed's comments. *Sounds exciting, but I've got a family and a responsible job to think about now. I certainly haven't got time to go gallivanting half-way across the world to catch up with someone we knew briefly, more than a decade ago.* 'So, it doesn't sound like Mo's coming, then'.

Luke confirmed this obvious deduction with another nod of the head. He had already declared his own intentions, despite his reservations, by bringing along some flight details and prices. He produced a crisp, brown envelope and placed it on the table in front of them. 'I've listened but a part of me thinks it's worth going,' Luke pronounced, gingerly.

'What part of you is that, then'? Saul threw back at him, sarcastically. 'You suddenly sound keen.'

'Just got a feeling that something good will come from this'. I'm owed three weeks holiday, so I could manage a ten-day trip. How about you, Saul?'

His friend had gone unusually quiet. 'Not sure, squire. There's something about this that doesn't quite ring true for me.' He was feeling more than a little reticent about giving it the go-ahead.

'Come on, Saul, it might be fun', Luke protested, more earnestly.

'I'll think about it.'

'Sarah might turn up in a few minutes; and who knows, maybe, even Gurdeep. Let's see what their take on it is.'

Sarah had finally got around to contacting Alan, a few days before the meeting at the pub. She shared later with Luke that when she heard Alan's voice, it felt, in an instance, as if those passing years had just melted away, like the sudden thaw of newly fallen snow, revealing the glow of a once familiar object. They talked for almost thirty minutes of some of the good times they had experienced back then. Although never romantically attracted to Alan, Sarah had treated him fondly, like a sister looking out for her younger brother. In truth, both were the same age, Sarah barely two months his senior. She was careful to avoid the topic of his early departure from university, but Alan was more at ease describing his late evolution into adulthood and the strange set of circumstances that had led to his regular trips to Eastern Nepal. He seemed really pleased to hear from her and talked ecstatically about his plan to bring together the flat-mates for a re-union in Nepal. Sarah finished by promising him that she would give the idea some serious thought.

Just after seven-thirty her once familiar face breezed into the bar. Time had gently modified her features, but there was no denying the distinctively cropped, permed blond hair and the confident Irish accent. 'Hi, guys, long time no see!'

Saul bellowed in her direction, 'Hey, Sarah. Great to see you. You look terrific.'

The two men greeted her enthusiastically, with a polite kiss on the cheek. Apart from carrying a little extra weight, she looked much as they remembered her. Her eyes still sparked with expectancy. 'I guess I'm surviving and all that stuff', she exclaimed vaguely.

'So, are you married yet? Saul enquired with his usual directness.

'Jesus. No!', came a tart response 'and before you ask, I haven't succumbed to motherhood either!'

The men grinned but didn't look surprised.

Although he hadn't seen her for ten years, Saul was still in the mood to wind her up. 'I find that a bit strange, Sarah, given your obvious maternal attributes!'

Saul's comment provoked the expected gesture from the now, rather stern-faced woman, standing in front of him. She pretended to deliver a slap across his cheek, but instead, shoved him gently in the ribs and laughed. Sarah reminded herself that he had 'held a candle for her', back in those days. Unfortunately for Saul, the feeling was not mutual. Although she felt a little flattered to receive such compliments, her tone was playfully cautious.

'No, I'm still looking for Mr Right, fellas. How about you two?'

Saul looked at Luke and the silence couldn't prevent Sarah enquiring, with a mocking grin, whether they had abandoned the pursuit of female partners in favour of a relationship with each other. 'Only joking lads, but you still look so good together. Peas in a pod!'

When the laughter subsided, Luke told her about Debbie and Ellen. Sarah listened intensively and awkwardly, offered what words of support she could.

Saul was less forthcoming about his personal life and was content with some banal comments about still not wanting to settle down yet. Sarah looked at them both and remarked that it didn't look as if any of them, including her, had moved on much in their personal lives, during the last decade.

Luke headed towards the bar to get Sarah a large glass of red wine. As he ordered the drinks, another voice from the past interrupted his train of thought. 'Hello, Luke. How are you?'

At first, he hardly recognised the Asian woman in a dark, formal suit and coat, but as she smiled, Luke realised he was looking at Gurdeep. Traces of grey hair had begun to compete with the once, vivid black strands, he remembered enveloping her head. Gurdeep stood there, motionless. She had immediately spotted him at the bar, as she walked into the lounge.

'I'm fine. And how about you', he blurted. 'The last I heard, you were working at some chemical company, in the city.'

'Yes, plastics, actually. I'm still there, trying to put all that scientific knowledge in my head to some use'. Gurdeep summoned the words with a glimpse of nervous laughter.

After purchasing an additional Orange and Passion-fruit for the latest arrival, they walked around the alcove to meet the others. Although pleased to see Gurdeep, they too, were also a little startled by the appearance of their latest visitor. She looked noticeably older. And none of them had expected her to turn up.

Gurdeep and Sarah swopped stories about what they had been doing over the last decade. The former had secured a good career at *Johnsons*, one of the largest chemical companies in the UK. None of the others were surprised. They remembered her as a dedicated and industrious student. There was little doubt in their minds, that she would do well. Why wouldn't she be successful, with all that ability? In fact, Gurdeep, or Dr Pavreen, as she now was, had done better than she could have ever hoped for.

For the first time ever she seemed prepared to share details of her background, growing up in Northern India and coming to Britain, two years before she started her degree. When Sarah asked if she was still in contact with her family, Gurdeep looked uneasy and simply answered 'No'. Eventually, she blurted out that 'Things got difficult at home and I needed to get away.' She eulogised about the kindness of a family she had got to know in Mumbai; their willingness to take her in and give her paid employment at their vegetable store; their assistance in putting her in contact with relatives they had in London when she expressed a desire to settle there. These were no more than a few pieces of a much bigger jigsaw; selected dates from a timeline, that Gurdeep was prepared to share with them, that evening. The absence of further details confirmed their view at the time, that this chapter of her life was still largely unavailable for extended discussion.

As if to deflect away from her identifiable tension, she mentioned some of her social interests. Art classes, trips to the theatre and a continued interest in Punjabi cooking, all tripped off her tongue. She threw in visiting galleries, museums and restaurants, in a somewhat vain attempt to dress up a social life that was something more than it really was. The others were not fooled.

There was no mention of a partner.

Sarah, on the other hand, was much less guarded. She spoke with them that she'd recently moved from Local Authority employment, to take up a private sector role supporting young offenders. The impact of nine years spent trying to protect vulnerable children within an inner London Local Authority, south of the Thames, had left its mark. Her decision to leave wasn't, she explained, because of the trauma of a broken shoulder that had never properly healed, sustained in her second year of service, after an altercation with an angry father. Nor was it the regular bruises and virulent abuse endured, almost daily, when she and her colleagues attempted to maintain a protective ring around the frighteningly high number of children at risk of abuse.

After leaving university, her initial employment had taken her through a probationary period as a Social Worker. Buoyed by the confidence gained at her degree placements, Sarah threw everything into her work. This was her mission. To challenge the deprivations and injustices that many young people endured; a vocation to root out the harm unleased by the domestic failures of their significant adult influences. As always, Sarah did not tread carefully, or diplomatically. She never minced her words. While other colleagues focused upon the abject poverty that sometimes provoked such neglect, Sarah believed that there were no excuses for a failure to nurture children properly and give them the same opportunities as others. 'Maybe', she joked 'That's why I found myself dealing with so many controversies! You remember me, always straight to the jugular.'

The others looked at her and it occurred to each of them, that Sarah hadn't changed at all in the years that had passed. They rather liked that about her.

Nine years of constant battling and two written reprimands had finally made her realise something. She described it like attempting to build up layers of progress by stacking precariously baked grains of sand upon each other and watching them fall back to the ground again. The bricks and walls of progress that they supposed to turn into, were just not strong enough. That was why she felt so frustrated. Confronting volatile parents, who were often angry at the accusations of neglect, responding with harsh words and actions, was a recipe for trouble. Those entrusted with the task of monitoring and supporting her work, began to lose patience with her more direct and sometimes, controversial approaches. Diplomacy and compromise were not strong features of her strategy. Her blood pressure had begun to rise to worryingly high levels, not helped by copious amounts of wine, consumed, then, on most days of the week. Eventually, she found herself looking at what she believed might be a safer refuge for her sanity; somewhere her skills and expertise could re-energise an ability to make a difference. Sarah was now six months into her new job: assisting young offenders, with their re-integration into society. It seemed to be generating fewer inner tensions, even if the work was just as challenging.

Her current employer was a private company franchised by the Government, to work with young men in danger of re-offending and spending most of their lives in prison. The day to day organisation was more chaotic, but she quite liked that. 'Fewer prying eyes and layers of bureaucracy. Most of the young men, I try to help are receptive to support and I've got some empathy with their struggle to cast aside their criminal past. After all, if things had turned out differently, it might have been me sitting in front of the probation officers and support staff. I'm now as professionally content as I'm ever likely to be.'

The conversation moved onto the subject of Alan. Both women had come to an initial decision about the proposed trip. Gurdeep repeated that she was unlikely to take up the offer and even if she could, she didn't really have any leave left for the rest of the year. 'Anyway, I would want to have much more detail about what we were supposed to be doing before I could sign up to such an enterprise! But, I have to say it's been lovely to see you all again, after such a long time'.

'Oh, Gurdeep, come on! I can't go out there without you!', Sarah remonstrated, with a persuasive arm around her shoulder.

Half an hour later, all the former flat-mates rose to go their separate ways. Luke and Sarah were still keen to go to Nepal. Saul remained hesitant but didn't rule out the possibility. Only Gurdeep indicated that she wasn't particularly keen to go. They assumed that Mohammed had already made his decision.

13

A fish out of water

Alan mopped his brow and retreated from the noise and dirt of the dusty street. The sanctuary of a local tourist bar was always inviting. A large glass of local beer would distract him from the oppressive heat, at least for a few minutes. As was his manner these days, he quickly engaged in conversation with those around him. The bar was packed with a mixture of European, American and Australian trekkers, local businessmen and various artisans from the nearby districts of central Kathmandu. The local workers were the ones he preferred to engage in conversation. In truth, the indigenous Nepalese were not too sure what to make of this maverick from the UK. They were used to many kinds of foreigners: obsessed climbers chasing the glory of Everest success, hardened trekkers following ancient tracks in hidden valleys; business men, with an eye for new products or trade deals in exotic plants and hard woods. Even traders looking for the next big market. Someone had tried to sell him small worms with aphrodisiac qualities from the high slopes of certain hill regions! There was something for everyone to buy here. Alan, however, didn't quite seem to fit into any of these categories.

Despite their initial reservations about him, he didn't take long to ingratiate himself into their company. Alan had fallen in love with this northern frontier of Asia and the contrasting lives of her people; their religious beliefs, practices and customs. He patiently listened to them articulating their philosophies and hopes for the future. When he spoke to those whose homes were high up in the Himalayan villages, he sensed that such communities still held on to traditions which outsiders, like him, would find it difficult to understand. Whenever he had the chance, he would travel beyond the capital city to see for himself. In the isolated communities, sandwiched between towering peaks, he encountered great warmth among the inhabitants. He was fascinated by their remote, enigmatic lifestyles. Slowly but surely, he was learning to adapt the land of Nepal as his spiritual home.

He often laughed, when he found himself making proclamations on this subject. 'Me, the most secular of creatures, drawn to a region of the world where the earth and heavens seem to collide. Where earning money is only the means to make life more manageable. A place where a man can understand himself against the awesome power of the earth. If only my folks could see me now!' They wouldn't have understood though.

Within the tranquillity of all this, he needed to be reminded that, like everywhere, there were real worries and challenges to be met. Lack of high quality education, health care and the constant dangers of natural disasters, still visited these regions with the impact of an apocalypse or medieval plague. People spoke about their constant fear of Nepal's two great neighbours, China and India. Each undermining the status of this poor country where life for many rural people was a daily struggle to survive. But down here, in Kathmandu, Alan, was perceived as just another eccentric Englishman trying to 'find himself'.

But he was different. Alan was someone who wanted to listen; to hear about the joys, as well as the concerns of local families. Here was a man who was more than happy to buy locals drinks, but did not appear to be noticeably, well off. His appearance bordered on what some would label 'scruffy' for a westerner; an argument strengthened by the evidence of his ill-fitting jackets and well worn, faded khaki shorts. Of course, he could have fitted himself out with designer gear if he had wanted to. Even his boots were now looking like they had been discarded by a Sherpa guide who had just been paid and wanted others to recognise his newly purchased footwear by discarding his old ones to a friend!

Alan's indigenous acquaintances did not know this, but that was exactly how he preferred them to think about him.

He had other things on his mind. The following day he was heading out to the Annapurna range to initiate something monumental.

14

Hobson's Choice

Gurdeep arrived earlier than usual the following day, with the sun still preparing to penetrate the night sky. There was already some commotion in the staff area. One of her team was scrutinising the notice board with some diligence. There was concern written across her face. 'Gurdeep. Have you seen this?' Her attention was drawn to a management memo occupying a prominent section of the board.

The managerial board of Jacobs Plastics Ltd. respectably draw your attention to an opportunity to take an attractive redundancy package available due to re-organisation of staffing at its London branch.'

At first, Gurdeep dismissed the implications that lay beneath the offer. As Head of the Research Centre, this surely wouldn't affect her, or the small team of scientists who assisted her. After all, it was barely six weeks since their widely publicised breakthrough in robotic plastics. When she came across one of her colleagues later that morning in the coffee area, she quizzed Rachel about the announcement. The other woman sighed, frustrated, and indicated that had she rather hoped that Gurdeep could elucidate more information on the matter. The Head of Research agreed to try and find out more, but it only added to the growing concern by staff that all was not well at the company.

Although a couple of colleagues put their names forward to accept the package and move on, this was clearly not the number the board was expecting or hoping for. Within two weeks, the news that everyone was dreading, emerged. The shock waves numbed the bones of Gurdeep's small, development unit and all who worked there. There were to be compulsory redundancies.

It took Gurdeep several days to digest the news she received the following day. Mr Cooper, the Chief Executive had summoned her to a meeting later that Tuesday, to be told that the research centre was to be closed. To be more accurate, it would be moved to another site. At first, she found the pronouncement bewilderingly difficult to process. How could they have reached such a decision? All the indications were that her section was doing well. Meeting all expectations.

The senior manager cleared his throat and began to explain that there had been developments.

When Gurdeep sat down later at home, with a cup of strong, black tea to help soothe her thoughts, she reflected on Cooper's words.

'Over-stretched borrowing figures; urgent need for new research funding; new Chinese backers; new factory location; reduced costs; an opportunity to move to Beijing...' The result of all this seemed something of an impossible choice. They wanted her and her team to move to China. Well that simply wasn't going to happen. She thought about the passport she had bought in Mumbai, more than a decade ago. It would run out in less than twelve months. Would she be as fortunate when she tried to renew it? No-one had queried the validity of her status in the UK. That could change. She had good reason to avoid unnecessary travel to other countries. Even after all these years, she wondered if she could still be deported back to India? The thought made her anxious, in a way she hadn't felt for a long time. Going to China was too much of a risk and the truth was she didn't want to live there anyway.

The Plastics Group would just have to replace her; maybe the whole team?

She caught sight of her image in the mirror on the wall. Gurdeep saw the reflection of an older woman; more like the image of her mother. Someone, who had possibly given too much of herself to her work. Was she ready to start all over again, on a foreign shore, so far away from her British life?

She blew hot air onto the bathroom mirror and defiantly wrote the word 'No' with her finger.

15

Temptation calls

Mohammad sealed the data sheet inside the envelope and placed it in the tray next to the picture of his wife and boys. He looked at his watch. Lunch was increasingly becoming a problematic luxury, to fit into his packed, working days. But he knew he had to eat. Although still a little early, his eyes needed a rest from the constant glare of his computer screen. Sometimes, it felt like the screen physically grew larger as the day progressed, eventually appearing like one of those giant TV's that adorned the walls of many pubs and restaurants, with their continuous diet of sport. However, the words he read seemed to be getting smaller. Maybe, it was time to make that appointment with the optician's, which he had been putting off for months.

He walked over to the elevator and stopped. He recalled a promise he'd made to himself, three days earlier, at the start of the month. Daily exercise! As he began to ascend the first flight of stairs, Mohammed was conscious about how sluggish he was becoming in his movements. Early thirties and moving around like a man twice his age! He couldn't even offer obesity as an excuse, as somehow, he'd maintained a reasonable weight over the years. He never used to be so inactive. All that tennis and squash he used to find time for, had slowly been squeezed out of his life. The stairway was a relatively small gesture of defiance against the gathering lethargy of middle age sloth.

On reaching the fourth floor, and noticeably out of breath, he made a mental note to visit that gym in town later, where he was still a paid -up member. And hopefully, more than once this month! If for no other reason the cost of his occasional visits just didn't make financial sense.

Mrs Jackson was standing in front of the hot trays at the entrance of the canteen. She always was at 12.30pm. He wondered if she ever went home. 'Hello Mo. You're early today. How are you?', she bellowed confidently. He liked the way she effortlessly seemed to remember almost everyone's name. They had, however, both worked at the company for several years.

'Got some nice vegetarian quiche over here', she said, stirring the vegetables. Her rounded cheeks broke into a broad smile as she proudly directly his gaze towards her latest gastronomic creation.

'How could anyone refuse?', he retorted, playfully and did not offer any resistance to the copious slice of tart she placed upon the plate. There was hardly any room for the jacket potato and mixed salad that he hastily lifted onto its edges. He liked May Jackson. She was such a cheerful soul in a micro-environment of serious attitudes, deadlines and constant pressures that surrounded her customers. This was Corporate Finance after all. He wondered if it was being surrounded by the touch and smell of freshly cooked food that raised her spirits, or was it the absence of mountains of tedious paperwork in her work that allowed her such a happy disposition? Whatever it was, it fuelled an attitude he could warm to, even escape to, for twenty minutes on a good day. The food was also delicious.

It was only when he sat down at the table that he noticed somebody looking at him. This was not the casual glace afforded to a passing pedestrian that one might encounter in the street. Mohammed looked across again, to the table next to the outside window. 'Somebody else in need of an early lunch today, then', the person called across. The voice belonged to a tall, elegant man, in a light blue suit. His strong features blended to create a handsome image. For a moment something stirred within Mohammed. He turned towards the colleague who had called over to him and found himself, rather awkwardly, staring back at the young man. This was more than just a polite gesture. He composed himself to avoid blushing with embarrassment.

Mohammed thought he vaguely recognised him. From some inter-department meeting in the recent past? The man broke into a pleasant smile and introduced himself. 'I'm Tarek by the way, from Marketing'.

His dining companion was still looking at him, but his gaze had wandered downwards. Tarek moved across from his table, still carrying his chicken lunch and sat next to Mohammed. An enticing hint of morning after-shave made the older man's nostrils momentarily twitch. Tarek looked into Mohammed's eyes and beyond; calmly opening that old locked door that lay buried in Mohammed's conscience. He smiled again and asked, 'How are things were in Sales?'

A touch of panic now consumed Mohammed. How could this stranger possibly know his secret? He had fastidiously guarded this reality for so long; from family, friends, even his wife, Fatima. Yet this work colleague, whom he hardly knew, had sat down in front of him and appeared to have cast aside the façade with no more than a glance.

They ate in an awkward silence. Tarek finished his meal and stood up to leave. 'See you around sometime', he said. Mohammed responded with an acknowledging gesture and watched his colleague move towards the exit. He guessed he was about twenty- five, some seven or eight years younger than himself. He sat and tried to compose himself for a few seconds. What did he mean by that phrase, 'See you around?' At work? In the canteen? Somewhere else? Somewhere more intimate? His mind was racing but he quickly gathered his senses, realising it was time to head back to the office. He spent most of the afternoon thinking about Tarek. None of these thoughts were conveyed to, or could be shared with anyone that evening, especially not with Fatima.

The following day was a wet and listless one, characterised by heavy clouds and faded light. Mohammed found himself scrolling down the list of company employees at A. R. Investment Enterprises. He clicked on to 'Marketing' and there, half-way down the page, was the image of Tarek. The gentle smile had been replaced with a sterner, more professional pose, but there was no mistaking the attractive image of his lunchtime companion. It occurred to him in that moment that he felt like doing something monumentally dangerous. As if compelled by an unstoppable force, his hand was already constructing a brief e-mail to the source of his fixation. Using the pretence of seeking advice about the marketing of a new investment package, he asked if he could visit Tarek to discuss this, the following day.

Tarek responded positively, within the hour and suggested an alternative venue. The canteen, at lunchtime. Precisely at the stroke of one o'clock, both men entered Mrs Jackson's house of nourishment and acknowledged each other with polite nods. Tarek sat down with Mohammed, his hand randomly brushing across his colleague's arm. A tinge of excitement shot through Mohammed's body.

They chatted about their work at the company and how they had come to be there. Both men seemed to understand the importance of the smokescreen that was being presented to the outside world. Mohammed thought it was telepathic! Towards the end of their meal, Tarek placed a small note in his hand and smiled invitingly. 'If you're interested?', was all he uttered, as he stood up and walked away to the door.

The Sales broker looked around carefully, to see if anyone was watching him, before opening the note. There was a telephone number written on the paper. Nothing else. Mohammed felt the urge to ring it instantly but tried to stay calm. He hadn't felt like this before. Ever.

After speaking on the phone that evening, the two men agreed to meet on Thursday, at a local pub. Mohammed arrived early. He needed to compose himself. Although he didn't normally drink alcohol, he felt compelled to order a glass of brandy at the bar. This was not going to be easy for him. The subsequent arrival of Tarek found him a little more relaxed than he dared to expect.

'You haven't done this much, have you, brother?', the younger man enquired.

Mohammed could barely look in his direction; frozen by the surreal reality of the moment. He managed to mutter something about difficult circumstances and lack of opportunities. He didn't sound convincing.

'How long have you been in denial?' Tarek whispered.

'I guess, all my life' he blurted. 'It's the culture, you know.'

He hadn't specifically asked him, but from his appearance and name, Mohammed had assumed Tarek was also from a Muslim background.

'The thing is Mohammed, this is London, man. You can be yourself here.'

His companion wasn't so sure about that.

Tarek explained that his parents had come to the UK from Bangladesh, in the nineteen-sixties, but quickly realised that to be accepted into the community they needed to compromise. They had continued to practice their faith and visited their local mosque in Birmingham but kept a low profile. The responsibilities of running a shop which hardly ever closed, kept all the family members busy. His father left most of the parenting duties to his wife. She emphasised that all three sons needed to assimilate into British society and instead of social activities at the mosque during weekends, Tarek and his brothers played football with the local boys and attended the youth centre.

All this contact with local kids created a platform for their adolescent adjustment to adult life and gave Tarek the freedom he needed to explore his sexuality. Even so, he needed to be careful. Too many suspicions would lead to pointed fingers and worse, if it was suspected that a Muslim teenager was entertaining notions of 'lying with another man.'

Mohammed sat quietly and absorbed all he heard. There was much in this he could relate to.

Tarek suggested they move on to a bar he knew well in the city. A short tube journey took them into an old part of town, with brightly painted buildings. One of these places was the 'Night Owl'. Immediately, Mohammed realised he had walked into a gay bar. A host of curious eyes fixed upon this unknown face. Tarek, however, seemed to know plenty of people there and introduced Mohammed to some of his friends. The two men took their drinks to a corner of the room and

Tarek sat closer to his companion. He ran his fingers gently through Mohammed's hair and kissed him on the cheek. Mohammed 's pulse almost exploded. Within seconds their lips had met. They embraced with the passion of impulsive teenagers. 'Let's get out of here', Tarek whispered in his ear.

Within the hour, they were writhing naked, on Tarek's bed, consumed with the passion of carnal discovery. Each touch made Mohammed quiver with excitement. His desire for his new partner's body was unquenchable.

Already, it was nine o clock.

'You know I'm married' he eventually said.

'I had guessed,' came the unruffled reply. 'To a woman, I assume.'

'Yes, and one who deserves better than this from me,' the older man retorted. He sat up and managed to hold back a tear that was starting to roll down one cheek, as he considered the implications of what had happened.

'Don't be too hard on yourself! Sometimes it takes courage to acknowledge your true feelings, my friend. The burden people like us carry within Islam, is to learn how to disguise these feelings, so that those we love may not suffer too much.'

Mohammed thought about Fatima and the boys and told Tarek he had to go. They dressed quickly, and Tarek watched, as his troubled companion left to consider how somehow, he would find a way to carry his new experience back into his other life.

Fatima was not pleased with him, when he stepped, gingerly, through the front door. 'What time do you call this? Where on earth have you been to this hour? and not so much as a message to let me know. Your dinner, or what's left of it, is in the oven, if you still want it!'

Mohammed had hurriedly rehearsed his story, during the drive home. 'Going for a drink with a friend from work' was unnervingly accurate, in the circumstances. The bit about not being able to find his phone, was less convincing.

'Sometimes, Mohammed, I don't know what you are thinking these days', she offered, frustratingly. Her husband, who had taken refuge in silence, eventually fumbled an apology in her direction.

Mohammed met Tarek on three other occasions during the next couple of weeks. Each time, he had 'popped' into his gym, as he promised he would do, but only stayed fifteen minutes. The physical activity he craved for would be found elsewhere.

Tarek had suggested they meet next time at the 'Night Owl' and Mohammed agreed, if somewhat reluctantly. He didn't really like the place and felt exposed to the glare of preying eyes. He had begun to get to know some of Tarek's acquaintances and friends but found their confidence and their bold assertiveness, difficult to deal with. They left the club and decided to walk through the local park. It was a beautiful late summer evening and the birds were already rehearsing their overtures to dusk. Mohammed was much more at ease in these surroundings and reached out for Tarek's hand. His companion smiled, and they sat on the local bench to absorb the flickering embers of another day's closure.

Mohammed knew in his heart, that his newfound happiness couldn't last. There were serious implications to consider. While he pondered the dramatic changes, the last few weeks had brought to his pedestrian existence, a fuse was about to be lit. It would blow his life apart. He didn't expect the hand which held the touch paper to come from such a close source.

While he enjoyed the sweetness of Tarek's touch, two bicycles had come to a halt on the elevated path, some way behind their park bench. A twelve- year old girl had removed her helmet to adjust her hair. Her father, on the other bike, took the opportunity to scan in the rich colours of a pre-autumn landscape. 'Dad! Look! Isn't that Uncle Mohammed over there.'

Fatima's brother, Javed, nonchalantly gazed across to the bench only to be visibly shaken by the sight of his brother-in-law in the process of kissing another man on the lips. He gazed at the spectacle with open-mouthed shock. Pulling himself together he tried to make his denial sound convincing. 'No! Haleema. It's just someone who looks like your uncle. Come on, we need to get back now. It's school tomorrow!' Javed hurriedly adjusted his cycle and implored his daughter to get moving. 'No, not this way! We'll head back through the other gate'

He was already deep in thought, grappling for the agonizing words he would need to break the heart of the sister he loved.

16

Exposure

Fatima was busy cleaning the cooker when the telephone rang. The sound of her brother's voice always raised her spirits. They got on well and had done since they were small children.

'Hi Fatima. How are you?' Her brother tried to disguise the heavy weight in his heart. 'There's something I want to talk to you about, Fatima'.

'Why not pop in later, when Mohammed is back from work? He'd love to see you.'

Javed breathed deeply to maintain his composure. 'I would rather chat to you on your own, sister.'

She laughed and teased him about his secretive tone. 'Is this something to do with Mohammed's birthday then, next week? A mysterious party gathering?'

Her brother's tone became more sombre. 'Not really. There's something I need to discuss with you, urgently. I can't talk about it on the phone now'

The siblings exchanged diary information about their movements over the next couple of days. There was a 'window' the following lunchtime and her brother agreed to call in during his break.

Javid arrived punctually at the appointed time. Friday's rainclouds painted a suitably gloomy back-drop to the message he carried. 'There is no easy way to say some things' he eventually blurted out after embracing his sister with a particularly firm hug. 'What I 'm going to tell you is so hard to share. I wish it was somebody else stood here before you.'

'Hey little brother, you're starting to scare me! What's happened? Has someone in the family died?'

Javed carefully recounted his trip to the park during his cycle ride with Haleema, the previous day. As the details of what they saw were articulated, Fatima's face dropped. Her expression juxtaposed from a look of insecure panic to one of utter disbelief. The trauma of such news tightened her features and stupefied her gaze. It was as if she metamorphosed into stone as the details emerged. This was followed by tears which descended from her eyes, each one expanding the pool of moisture coating her cheeks. Eventually, Fatima sank into the refuge of her sofa. 'No! No! Javed, it can't be true! There must be some other explanation for what you saw. Are you sure this wasn't just a couple of friends embracing, or some relative you didn't recognise?'

His sister could no longer be spared the raw facts. The explicit sexual messages observed on the park bench; the repetitive nature of her husband's kisses upon the lips of another man. Fatima tears had given way to anguished cries. Her pain was also bubbling up into anger.

'What on earth does he think he is doing?' The selfish bastard! My Mohammed, the father of our boys. Gay? I can't believe it!' In the silence which followed, Fatima scrutinised her mind, desperately looking to pull any relevant snippets of information from her memory. His recent late returns from work, the frequency of his late 'work meals', but most of all his reluctance to touch her in the way he once did. She tried to remember when they last had made love, or even when he last embraced her with noticeable passion. It had been some time.

Javed returned with tea from the kitchen. 'Are you okay?', he muttered as he offered the cup to her, realising how facile the question was.

'What are we going to do, Javed?' she finally ventured.

'We'll do what we always do in a crisis, sister. We will deal with it, as a family.'

Had Muhammed witnessed this conversation, his own demeanour would also have changed. Dealing with anything like this 'as a family' was the last thing he wanted.

That evening, the boys were in bed earlier than usual. Fatima had cooked dinner for herself and Mohammed, as usual, and the table was laid. As her husband turned his key in the lock, Fatima was already rehearsing her meticulously prepared words.

'Hi Darling. I'm home. What's for dinner. I'm famished!'

'Sit down, Mohammed. I need to speak to you.'

'Can't it wait to later.'

She ignored him and went into the kitchen, returning with a pot of chicken curry. With as much strength as she could muster, she threw the pot down in front of her startled partner, cracking his plate and sending his cutlery flying across the table. 'NO. IT CAN'T!

Fatima scoured every inch of her husband's face, to gauge his response to each accusing word she threw at him. She didn't hold back! This time the agonised facial features belonged to her husband. He squirmed and lowered his head as she interrogated him about his clandestine 'friend' in the park. He slid further down his chair as she insisted upon knowing whether they had slept together and exactly what they had done beneath the sheets. Each accusation, bellowed in his direction, was delivered with ever greater venom by his wife. 'How long, Mohammed. How long has this been going on?'

His feeble attempts to explain the circumstances of their initial meeting and the subsequent rendezvous, met with cold silence.

'So, what are we supposed to do now. Just tell me that!', she exclaimed.

He tried to explain that he had always struggled to suppress certain thoughts about other men. When he was a teenager, these 'demons' would come to him in the night, invading his sleep. Who could he possibly discuss these thoughts with? His father, a conservative Muslim, with little experience of such things, would have attempted to beat such sinfulness from him. The local Iman, at the mosque, would have subjected him to endless indoctrinatory dogma. It would take more than intense, extensive exposure to Koranic teaching on human relationships, for Mohammed to abandon his true sexuality. Most traumatic of all, he would be ostracised from the *Ummah* or Muslin community, banished from those he loved; tarnished with an unspoken label. 'That's why I kept those feelings secret from the women I met.' It was why he had engaged in the illusion of heterosexual attraction. He knew that one day he would take the sacred vows with someone like Fatima. His marital duty was to build a secure family; give her children. Had he not done this?

Mohammed begged her to try and understand all this and what had finally happened to expose the deception. He emphasised that he still loved her and of course it certainly didn't need saying, that he loved their boys with every fibre of his being. Fatima just stared at him, her heart shattered, like glass into a thousand pieces, each one a memory of the past that was unlikely to keep its place in an uncertain future.

Before slamming the dining- room door, she said, 'The family are coming around tomorrow night at seven, to discuss what happens next. You need to be here!'

Familiar faces had gathered at his house, by the time Mohammed arrived home from work the next day. Sat around the lounge like some sort of ancient tribal council, they cast their eyes with singular intent on the man they had thought they knew. There was his father, Ahmed, whimsically stroking his grey beard as

Mohammed's mother sat, uncomfortably, with head bowed. His uncle Ali was there too, a huge bull of a man, who sat next to his aunt. Both looked like arbiters of doom. His brother-in-law, Javed, sat next to Ali, glaring menacingly in his direction. Finally, the robed figure of the Iman, from their mosque, completed the group. Mohammed hadn't been to Friday prayers for several weeks now and avoided eye -contact with his clerical visitor.

'Quite a gathering', he eventually muttered. The accused sat down opposite his denouncers and waited for his 'trial' to begin. His father spoke first.

'How could you bring such shame upon your mother and I', he exclaimed, despondently. You have destroyed your family with this outrageous thing.'

Each of the others offered similar comments about the evil of what he had done and the implications for his immortal soul. Javed dwelt upon the impact of this behaviour upon his wife, Fatima and the humiliation he had brought upon her.

Mohammed tried to explain why this had happened. How sorry he was to hurt his wife and embarrass the family. They didn't seem to be listening. They certainly didn't want to understand.

'Cast aside this abomination and swear by Allah's messenger, Mohammed, whose name you bear, and have now disgraced, that this is the end of such nonsense', the Iman boldly announced.

It was all too much for Fatima, who rushed out of the room in tears, and headed towards her bedroom.

After an hour and a half of such interrogation, Mohammed told them he needed some fresh air and left the 'jury' to deliberate. Once outside the front door he walked and just kept on walking. He knew there was nothing he could offer in his defence. They would probably agree that he needed a break from the family to clear his head and focus on his responsibilities.

This castigated soul needed more than just a brisk walk to clear his mind.

He suddenly thought again about Alan and his offer. It might not be such a bad idea to join them after all.

17

Escaping the Rain

The unusually bedraggled figure of Saul Weiner pushed open the outside door of Wilson's IT Services and shook himself vigorously. He was hoping to dislodge at least some the surface rain water that had settled, unceremoniously, in every 'nook and cranny' of his fibre. Saul was in an agitated mood. He hated not 'looking his best' in front of people. The impact of this morning's torrential downpour, coupled with his inability to bring either a hat, brolly or even a waterproof coat, had carved the spectre of this sodden, drenched creature, standing before them.

'Been out for an early morning swim, Saul?', his colleague, John, called out, mockingly, as he stood there, dripping, unceremoniously. Saul's usually groomed hair was hanging across his face, limply, in disarray.

A more helpful member of the team threw him a green-stripped towel, to enable this saturated victim to begin repairing his public image. 'I hate this weather', he eventually announced to his assembled colleagues, in an irritated tone. 'It's only a ten-minute walk from the tube station and look at the state of me!' He switched his computer on and waited for his hair to recover from its dishevelled misery. He swigged from a refreshing cup of cappuccino from the drink's machine and took refuge in reading his e-mails.

There was a message waiting for him from Molly, in Human Resources. It appeared that his provisional enquiry about 'taking leave' in November was less problematic than he'd anticipated. In fact, such requests for holiday were being actively encouraged. He realised that if the truth be told, this was more about the annual headache of maintaining appropriate staffing levels throughout the summer months, than any desire to meet the individual needs of those who worked for the company. He thought again about Alan's proposal. It was starting to sound more attractive with each dreary October day.

Later that evening, he rang Luke, who was sounding chirpy. 'I've been firming up flight arrangements for Nepal. Any nearer to a decision, mate?'

Saul said 'I think I'm going to join you after all. Been checking out leave possibilities at work and it seems I have the 'green light'.

Luke could not disguise his pleasure with the news. 'That's brilliant, mate. We'll have a great time.'

'I still want to see more details from Alan', though, he interjected, as if to keep Luke's enthusiasm in check.

The friends arranged a final meeting at Luke's flat for the following week to share their thoughts about the trip. 'So, including the two of us, that's four going' said Luke.

'Don't you mean three?' Saul interrupted.

'Gurdeep has decided to come along now'.

'I thought she was adamant that it wasn't for her?' Saul probed.

'It seems that she's changed her mind. Something to do with work.'

'And I have news for you', Saul added. 'We're going to need a fifth ticket. Mohammed's coming too. He told me he need to get away from everything for a couple of weeks.'

Meanwhile, over in Nepal, Alan was beginning to comprehend the news that all five of his former flat-mates were now going to make the trip. He looked out upon his mountain wilderness, to catch the final flickers of daylight and permitted himself a moment of quiet satisfaction.

18

Decisions

Alan had finally sent out further details about the trip to his former flat-mates. It appeared that he had purchased a collection of buildings on the outskirt of a mountain village, close to somewhere called Upper Hepsang. When Saul and Luke scrutinised a map they found on-line, they were amused to see there was also a Lower Hepang, there too. Neither of them had heard of either, nor Humde, Dhikur Pokhara, or any of the other villages and towns scattered around the Northern ridges of the Annapurna mountains. There was little information to add to all this, except the name of a hotel. The 'Wheel of Life', in central Kathmandu, was where they were to meet Alan after they arrived. If he could greet them at the airport, he would try to do so. Failing, that, he would send someone to collect them.

Mohammed was the first to arrive on Tuesday evening for a meeting convened by Luke. He did not look well. Apart from the dark ridges under his eyes, his hunched shoulders and worried expression, suggested that recent days were proving quite a challenge to him.

Luke asked him if things were okay, reinforcing his welcome with a warm cup of tea and chocolate biscuit.

His visitor said he'd share his problems with them when they had all arrived and changed the subject quickly. 'So how about you, Luke, what have you been up to in the last ten years?'

His host rattled through some headlines of working within the export business, getting married, divorced, becoming a parent and still hanging out with Saul. Mohammed grew visibly more uneasy with his mention of domestic strife.

The others arrived in rapid succession. The atmosphere lifted with the cheery presence of Sarah and Saul, clearly looking forward to their imminent adventure. Gurdeep was more guarded and reeled off a list of urgent issues they should look at before they went home that night. Luke watched his guests mingling and smiled. Some of that old chemistry was still there, he thought. 'So Gurdeep, how come you changed your mind about going?'

The research chemist gathered her thoughts and told them what had happened. She played down her anger in favour of a more philosophical stance. 'After so long at the same place, I probably need a change and I certainly don't want to move to China.' She recounted the details of the planned re-location at work with meticulous detail, adding light-heartedly, 'Anyway, who's going to keep you boys out of mischief if I don't come along!'

Sarah laughed and mentioned that she certainly wasn't going to be their nursemaid on the trip.

They all sat around the kitchen table and in -between demolishing the content of Luke 's biscuit tin, examining the map Luke had bought on *Amazon*. 'This is where the place is.' Luke pointed to the unknown network of villages, lying in the shadows of Annapurna 'II' and 'IV.'

'Crikey! Talk about the middle of nowhere!', Sarah exclaimed. 'I'm glad we're not expected to make our own way there.'

Mohammed's mood had lifted with the unravelling of the Himalayan map. 'Magnificent! These mountains stretch thousands of miles, you know, as far as my grandfather's village in Pakistan. Can you believe that?'

The others thought they had uncovered a clue about why Mohammed was joining them. Was he intending to extend his trip to include a journey across to his grandfather's homeland? 'I don't think we're going to hike that far!' Saul volunteered.

'I'm not hiking anywhere, Gurdeep interrupted.' I thought this was a holiday?'

The conversation moved on to more practical issues. A whirlwind of suggestions about clothing, combating weather conditions, suitable medicines and language, ensued.

'How's your Nepalese, Gurdeep?' Saul enquired.

'She looked at him disapprovingly and told him that Nepal was a largely Hindu country. With my Hindi and your 'pigeon' English, Saul, I'm sure we will manage to communicate with the local people.'

The others laughed. Strange, Luke thought, how some things change so little over the years.

'Will I need malaria tablets?', Sarah asked.

'Not where we're heading, I shouldn't think, Saul retorted. 'The little buggers will find it far too cold up there!'

They turned their attentions to the information Alan had sent. He was suggesting that they fly out on Heathrow's regular scheduled early evening flight, on Sunday ninth of November, arriving at Kathmandu Airport at around midday on the Monday. Alan had already set up a payment for the tickets with British Airways. All they needed to do was to supply the airline with their full names, dates of birth and passport details. They could obtain their visas at the airport in Kathmandu. If Alan was unable to meet them at the airport, he would send someone to pick them up and drive them to the hotel. Rooms had already been provisionally booked for them. He would most likely meet them in the lobby area.

There followed a list of essential things for them to bring. Most of it was about keeping them warm. Although the day-time temperatures would be quite pleasant, once the sun went down, the late air would carry with it, a sharp, icy chill. This would descend across the valleys, swept along by strong afternoon winds and remind them that the Himalaya could offer a frosty welcome to those who visited her at night.

Alan was less forth-coming in his itinerary of what they were going to do each day. He had asked them for a little patience with this; it was taking time to assemble everything he needed.

'Well, I'm happy enough to cope with a few surprises,' said Sarah, belligerently.

'As long, as we're not going to be trapped there for ever', Saul said.

They made plans to meet at Heathrow, a little earlier than specified, to make sure the M25, the weather or both, didn't scupper their chances of getting there on time.

'I've got a good feeling about all this', Sarah announced to the others, as they made their way to the door. 'There's going to be some magic in this venture, you'll see!'

A recognisable scent of optimism could be detected in the room. Their initial anxieties had given way to growing confidence in the venture. This was gathering momentum, reinforced by the realisation that at all five ex-flatmates would be re-united again, travelling to Nepal to meet their enigmatic and generous host.

PART TWO

SHADOWS OF WISDOM

19

A city on the move

Luke twisted his crushed arm back into place and slowly opened his left eye. The other reluctantly followed suit. His fingers pushed away the caked evidence of an uncomfortable night's sleep. He looked around. It was still quiet. Most of the passengers were asleep, although the internal aircraft lights had now been switched on. Luke felt the pronounced creases in his cheek. They itched, but at least they were beginning to subside and return his face back to some semblance of normality. An aching neck only added to the discomfort. Straightening himself up in the seat, he squeezed the connecting muscle at the base of his neck and tried to massage the 'creak' away. Maybe the window would offer some distraction.

He looked out upon swirling mists and thick billowing clouds. They saturated the skyline, enveloping the wing of the plane, which was intermittently lit up by it's red, flashing lights. The outline of the engine suddenly broke through this swirling haze; reminding everyone, of its awesome power. At such altitude, the sound was hardly audible. But it's turbines buzzed confidently, as it projected the plane, like some majestic bird of prey, across the skies. As he continued to look out upon this blanket of white and grey, it began to break up, revealing isolated pockets of dramatic landscape, below. Luke imagined what a closer view would reveal.

Jagged edges of innumerable mountains standing tall, as if to greet his gaze. The lower ridges, decorated in carpets of Himalayan green pine, peppered across the lower valleys, like an army of painted match-sticks. Great spurs of ice and snow meandering down from their summits, held in place by uncounted numbers of ancient rocks. The contours of mighty waterfalls, cascading over dramatic precipices, providing life-giving energy to the fields below. He continued to look out of the window and thought he caught sight of the glimmer of frozen lakes. Some of these, like precious jewels of blue ice, mirroring a dazzling reflection of the sky above. Others, dark, foreboding, and partially hidden, where the sun would rarely penetrate; suspended between towering monoliths of grey and black. There would be glaciers down there, too. Although they were difficult to pick out from that height, he had seen pictures before. He thought he could detect a couple of them, twisting their way down the valleys. They would consume all that lay in their path; packed in frozen tubes of blackened ice and snow. Luke imagined them slowly powering their way down to the base of the mountains, ready to disgorge their stony secrets to inquisitive human gazes. He felt excited, yet humbled, by the sheer scale and majesty of it all.

Meanwhile, some of the others had started to stir. He sensed they were nearing their destination. Busy flight attendants started to pass tin-foiled breakfast packs to comatose passengers in front of them. He nudged Saul. His friend was spread-eagled across both seats, his long legs wrapped around the space in front of Luke's feet. The shadow of yesterday's stubble seemed to hang from his face, like a man preparing the bristles of a new beard. His breath reeked of the remains of yesterday's sustenance. There were plenty of other early morning odours competing for air space on the plane. One of his least favourite moments, he mused, about over-night flights! The smell of tired feet and unwashed bodies competed for prominence with the sweet scent of chapatis and fruit being handed out by the cabin staff. He leaned across Saul and greeted Sarah and Gurdeep in the adjacent seats. 'Morning ladies! I think I need to shuttle across and use the toilet before the breakfast trolley traps me in here for another thirty minutes.'

A barely awake Gurdeep acknowledged him. Luke managed to galvanise Sarah into vacating her end-seat, so he could get to the isle. She too was ready to stretch her legs. It had been a while since she had been on a long flight like this and sitting still for so long was proving quite a challenge. 'Think I'll go too, before everyone else has the same idea', she announced, before ambling down to the back of the plane. Luke eventually managed to climb over the human obstacle course that barred his way and followed her to the toilets.

Meanwhile, the snoring behind his seat suggested that Mohammed had faded back into the comfort of sleep. 'Wakey, Wakey, my sleeping beauty.' Luke managed to reach between the seats to shake his arm.

Mohammed slowly returned to the land of the conscious. 'What time is it?' he enquired, in a disorientated voice.

'Time for breakfast, my friend' It's eight o' clock.'

The puzzled face of a jaundiced looking Mohammed appeared through the gap.

'We must be nearly there, then', he muttered, hopefully.

Fortified by the delights of a *British Airway's* breakfast, the weary travellers prepared to face Kathmandu Airport, a place sometimes described as an experience to be treasured, or stored in the memory banks, under exotic but said by others to be better avoided! As soon as the plane door opened, the full kaleidoscope of Nepalese culture was waiting to overwhelm them with its colours, noise and expectancy. Even Gurdeep, with memories of growing up in rural

Punjab, struggled to absorb the impact. There are nearly thirty million people living in Nepal and, as they cleared passport control and completed visa requirements, it seemed as though most of them had turned up at *Tribhuvan International Airport* that morning. Unfortunately, the person they most wanted to see, Alan, was nowhere to be found. In fairness, he had warned them that he might not be able to meet them in person.

They waited around for a short time after clearing customs, but soon grew tired of fending off the army of porters who wanted to carry their cases for a good price.

'He definitely said that someone would meet us at the airport if he couldn't be there himself', Sarah reminded them.

The consensus though was not to wait any longer and by the time they had struggled to the exit doors of the airport and started looking for a taxi to jump into, their patience was running a little thin. Then with perfect timing, Gurdeep drew their attention to a large sheet of white card, held aloft by an anxious looking, wiry man, with two protruding front teeth. The card reassuringly bore their names, written in large black letters.

Welcome to Nepal Luke -Gurdeep- Saul- Sarah and Muhammed

'Look over there! The sign!' They tentatively approached the bearer to be greeted with a huge smile from the old man. It became clear that the two exposed teeth were the only ones still present in his mouth.

'Namaste! Welcome, English friends! My name is Ram. Hope you had good journey. Alan meet you at hotel. Please. Come with me. I have taxi van.'

They trundled through a maze of old, brightly coloured buses, until Ram stopped at a large battered -looking green saloon van. Several dents had altered the front of the vehicle; one, having completely taken out the left headlamp. A flimsy wire hung limply, in the cavity, attached to a single bulb.

As Sarah turned around, there were still two teenage boys, seemingly attached to her luggage by super glue. Fifty *rupees* to each finally secured the release of their cases. She realised that the transaction had cost her the equivalent of less than a pound and felt a little embarrassed.

The journey into the centre of Kathmandu should have been a short one. Unfortunately, even five kilometres can take nearly an hour, when competing with half a million other road users. And that doesn't include the bicycles, cows, chickens, dogs and other life-forms, battling for space. As they looked out at the apparent chaos that surrounded them, it was hard to imagine that the city once stood at the centre of the most lucrative trade route in the world. Luke remembered something he'd read in his travel guide. For more than a thousand years, merchants had travelled through here from Tibet, heading on towards India, to peddle their goods. What a sight those caravans must have been to behold. Now, the city looked more like a vast, sprawling mass of mixed humanity. Many of them, no doubt, were competing for the higher wages available in the city. The people in Kathmandu, like other large conurbations, were drawn from many parts of Nepal, looking to build a future that subsistence farming was never going to compete with.

Like most travellers to this capital city, they headed towards the district of *Thamel*, close to the centre. A frenzied mix of hotels, bars, café's, clothing stalls and souvenir shops, dominated the surrounding buildings. They were close. However, there was one final reminder of the volatile nature of travel here, when they all ground to a sudden halt. It wasn't encouraging to see the drivers of some vehicles in front of them, leaving their transport and casually strolling down the middle of the road to chat to each other.

'We might as well stretch our legs too' Luke ventured. 'This doesn't look like a five-minute delay.'

As they stepped out of the car, each of them was hit by the suffocating odour of traffic pollution. Grabbing tissues, they quickly covered their mouths from the invading smog and fumes.

'God, What a stench!' Mohammed shouted. Spluttering coughs around us, acknowledged the impact of these pungent fumes.

'No wonder so many of these people are wearing masks', Saul added.

The humidity and intense heat only added to their collective discomfort.

'I'm retreating to the AC', Sarah shouted and Gurdeep joined her back in the car.

'What's going on, Ram?', Luke enquired.

'No problem. No problem. Important person coming through. Maybe government men. Short delay.'

Another ten minutes went by. The driver of the car in front was now sitting down in the middle of the road eating, what looked like his lunch.

'Daal bhaat tarkaari', Ram laughed. 'This is national dish. Has good wife to feed him! Yes?'

The appearance of successive cartons of rice, lentils, curried vegetables and pickles, confirmed their worst suspicions. These concerns had nothing to do with the food or his wife. They were all going to be there a while yet.

Eventually, after most of them, including Luke, had taken refuge in a midday snooze in the van, excited voices suddenly changed the atmosphere. Gurdeep, still awake, announced the arrival of three black Mercedes, flanked by several extremely loud and ostentatious motorbikes. Two overlapping red pennants, with symbols of the sun and moon, were fixed strategically to the vehicles. The national colours of red, blue and white, boldly fluttered from their wing mirrors, in an impressive show of State pride. Once they had passed, a cacophony of horns and roaring engines greeted the policeman's signal. Like the starting grid at a grand prix race, the mass of traffic revved up, then moved as one through the junction, with as much speed as they could muster. Strangely, everybody looked relaxed, despite the delay.

Alan's visitors were too tired to be exasperated. All they wanted was to see a hotel sign that said, *The Wheel of Life*, and soon. Finally, almost two hours after setting off, the neon lights of their accommodation appeared ahead, lighting up the afternoon sky. They turned off the main road and pulled into the hotel car-park. They looked a seriously bedraggled group.

'Come inside, please. They are waiting for you,' Ram bellowed.

The *Wheel of Life* had certainly 'gone to town', in reinforcing its name throughout the entrance area. Several large painted symbols adorned the furnishings and fittings. In the foyer, the whole west wall was draped with a giant collage of interlocking pictures. At its centre lay an image of three animals: a cock, a snake and a pig. Each chasing each other's tail. Circling these, was another set of images: creatures falling and rising through death and re-birth. Around these figures, six more pictures of things that could be described are impermanent, or non- lasting. A saintly figure or *Bodhisattva* held out a gift to the beings. Twelve inter-locking links surrounded the pictures, showing that all thoughts, words and actions, have consequences. There was an image of the Buddha himself, set apart from the wheel, standing above it, pointing towards the moon. At the top, the figure of a menacing demon looked down upon the whole spectacle.

'Fascinating,' exclaimed Mohammed, attempting to mask his ignorance.

'His name is Yama', said Gurdeep, confidently, clearly familiar with the symbolism. He is the demon who holds the wheel of life. He is the lord of death. He is holding a mirror up to life, reflecting the suffering around birth, death and re-birth.'

'Please tell me this is just a story', Sarah joked.

'Don't worry, I'll keep him away from you!'

The reassuring comment came from a bearded man standing behind them. He was not instantly recognisable as he should have been.

'Alan', exclaimed Sarah, hesitantly, staring at the man. 'Is that you?'

20

Gathering of old friends

A frenzy of huddled embraces and hand-shakes ensued, before they all sat down with a glass of mango juice in their hands, to start catching up on the events of more than a decade. It would take some time! Although, Alan looked a little older, especially with his recently grown straggly beard, his eyes glazed brightly. He looked tanned and relaxed. Alan welcomed them in a confident manner.

Luke broke the silence with a feeble attempt at humour. 'Well, I don't know what you've been taking recently, mate, but it's certainly agreeing with you'. 'I hope it's legal!'

'You'll find a lot of things here are good for you, Luke. And as far as the law goes, there are fewer regulations to worry about, in Nepal. People look towards the ground, towards each other, as much as they do towards the skies, for guidance about what is right. But more than that, they look towards their inner selves. One of the influences of the Buddha was to challenge us to take responsibility for our own lives, find a middle way to enlightenment, just as Gautama himself did'

The others listened attentively. Alan's voice carried a tone of authority that they didn't recognise. A touch of incredulity pervaded the moment. After all, this was Alan talking. As for Luke, he wished he hadn't said anything.

Their host certainly seemed different. As if monitoring their mood and needs with hidden tracker devises, their host implored them to hold on to their questions until later. Rest and refreshment was what they needed at this juncture. It didn't take sixth sense to realise that. Smartly dressed porters in ornate yellow and red jackets, led the weary travellers to their rooms to relax and freshen up. Their cases were already standing outside their doors, as they climbed the stairway. They would meet up again at seven for dinner. Alan assured them that he would answer more of their questions then.

A clearer picture of what they had agreed to participate in began to take shape, as the group re-assembled later, in the hotel restaurant. Everyone was ready to eat. It had been a long day. Their host had ordered something stronger than mango juice for them to drink, this time. Local beers and rice wine were waiting on the table. As they arrived, Alan was already seated. He was not alone. A stout man, of maybe forty, with curly black-hair and dressed in a traditional *Daura Suruwal* suit, sat next to him. He cut an impressive figure with his knee-length sleeved shirt, tied and closed at the side. He smiled sagely, but said very little, other than to greet them with a polite *Nameste.*

On Alan's left was an older woman, with distinctly Tibetan features, inquisitively gazing in our direction. None of them wanted to ask the obvious question about who they were. Better to wait to be introduced. It didn't take long. 'This…' said Alan, directing his gaze towards the woman next to him, '…is Dohna. She is also, like you, a long way from home. A Tibetan refugee, from over the Chinese border. She now lives at my house in the mountains. She is also known by the name of Dexa. It means '*to teach*'.

Dexa nodded and offered them a reassuring smile.

'The gentleman on my right is Amit', he continued. 'It is no coincidence that his name means 'immeasurable, for that is what he truly is!'

The British guests looked bemused. Only Gurdeep had suspected the significance of what Alan had said. She too bore a name from an Indian religion. Names, she knew, were seldom chosen without careful consideration, in this part of the world.

Saul put down his beer and looked towards his host. 'So, tell us, Alan. How did you find us, after all this time?'

'Oh, it's not that difficult, these days, he beamed confidently. Between *Facebook*, *Twitter* and other bits of social media, we're never more than a few clicks away from contact, even when you're based in a place like this.'

Saul looked around. He'd never been in a place like this before.

Alan was hungry for news from his guests. Ten years can look like a life-time, when people slowly start to uncoil the details of what has happened to them, over such a period, of time and his appetite for learning what his old flatmates had been doing was insatiable. He absorbed each detail with meticulous attentiveness. In his head, he was assembling the names of several local people he wanted them to meet.

Dexa, likewise, listened with intense concentration. It looked to Luke like she was processing every detail; storing the information in her head for further analysis. One hour soon drifted into two.

Sarah, as usual, was firing out words like machine-gun bullets, as she talked about her work in the UK. The need for young offenders to be given another chance, was a dominant theme in her frantic sharing of this. Each comment she made, burned with conviction. Luke admired that about her. She didn't mention the fact that in her personal life she was still single.

Saul waxed lyrically about his changing vagrancies of fortune over the years; the vain attempts of his family to protect and foster his Jewish identity and his inability to settle down. Luke, more than most, knew that that was only half the story. All of them shared a weakness for edited testimonies.

Gurdeep's anger with her situation at Johnsons, bubbled to the surface of her general conversation, embellishing her words with bitterness and irritation. But that deeper sadness of which she rarely mentioned, still lay buried within her.

As for Luke, he spoke about the challenges of parenting a child from the distance of a home that he no longer shared with her mother. There was the frustration of watching the woman he once loved, nurturing his child with another man. The nightmare scenario that an estranged father sometimes feared; knowing that they might one day move far away, severing contact with him, for good. He didn't speak about his loneliness, or how the magical moments he clung on to had something in common. They were all in the past.

Mohammed said very little. He looked uncomfortable, surrounded by so much sharing of personal experience. A few superficial comments about his wife and boys and the never-ending saga of monetary investment, was as much as he would venture.

Alan just sat there, listening. An occasional glance to his left or right found his companions still in studious mode.

The vegetable curry meal that arrived brought much appreciated nourishment, washed down by imported red wine and bottles of local beer.

Afterwards, Alan stood up and spoke: 'My friends, I'm sure you are eager for more details about what we are going to do during the next ten days. In some ways, the little information you have received is also a blessing. For when we embark on our journey to my home, tomorrow, we will also be embarking on another journey: a journey of the heart and mind. I believe that what we do will both challenge and inspire each of us. I'm not attempting to brain-wash you into believing anything religious or spiritual. I just want to share a little of the happiness that has ignited my soul. Who knows, you might find something to bring home with you?

'Many years ago, we lived together in a student house. Some of you could be forgiven for thinking that this was a disappointing time for me. Not so. I didn't understand at the time, but it was a time of preparation. Failing to complete my degree forced me to grow up; to face up to who I was and what I wanted to do with my life. Far from being a dark time, I found something there I needed and valued; a new family, a community. The laughter and excitement we shared back in those days had been in short supply in my life, prior to this.'

He recounted the tragic story of his little brother; the burden of sadness that hung over his parent's house for years, while he struggled to make sense of what had happened. He had not shared this with any of them before. He continued, 'I've never forgotten the camaraderie, the fellowship you shared with me in London then, and I've not found it in my life since. That is, until now. It took an enormous piece of good fortune in South Africa and a charismatic Indian merchant, to point me in the direction of Nepal.

'I may not have lingered too long in your memories, during this past decade. But since we went our separate ways you have always been in my thoughts. Yes, I know we were all different. We were destined to embark upon different paths. But there was a special bond with you that has always been there for me. For that reason, I wanted to see you again and try and help you. At the end of the trip, you will decide if the experience has been worthwhile. I really hope it is.'

He sat down again. Sarah struggled to hold back a tear. The rest of them sat in silence, humbled by his declaration. Luke was racking his brain with the possibilities of what Alan meant by trying to help them.

Finally Alan informed them that they would be heading off early the following day, to his Nepalese home. Both Dexa and Amit would be accompanying them in the minibus. He begged their patience for what would be, in places, a long and arduous journey. 'Oh, and don't sit in the middle of the back seat. Not if you are a delicate traveller! The suspension in the mini-bus has seen better days! We will probably need to stay over in Pokhara, or somewhere close to it, which is seven or eight hours away! I'll arrange this, later. Then, of course, there's the weather. Things can be a little precarious at this time of year, but don't worry. We'll get there eventually.'

He cushioned the impact of his statement with a big, confident smile, before continuing. 'Before we even begin to think about that, we've got to battle through the traffic in Kathmandu. Always a struggle, unfortunately,' he exclaimed, as you have already experienced. But at least these are proper roads in this section of the journey. Once we get beyond Besi Shamar, to the Marsyangdi River Valley, we'll really slow down, as we hit the gravel tracks. In fact, we will also need to walk a little, too, as we get nearer to my home at Upper Hepsang. Have you all brought walking boots and waterproof jackets and hats as I suggested?'

The visitors all nodded.

Luke looked out of the window and observed the sweltering spectacle of a hot and steamy Kathmandu evening. It occurred to him that some might think this a strange request. The sun, which had beamed down on them without mercy that day, looked set to repeat its ferocious drama again, on each subsequent day.

Gurdeep mumbled something about not being built for hill walking but had read enough about the Himalaya mountains to realise the lunacy of ignoring such advice about appropriate equipment.

Amit asked them if he could see their walking kit, to ascertain if they needed to add to it, before entering the Annapurna Conservation Area. 'A beautiful, but dangerous place', he added, as if to emphasise the point. 'Nothing can be left to chance, up there.'

Saul and Mohammed returned from their rooms with rucksacks, boots and gloves for their kit inspection. It was the first time Mohammed had broken into a big grin since arriving. 'Like camping with the scouts, again,' he smirked.

Saul, always the alpha male, presented his gear with competitive pride. 'That's a '£200 jacket, there. *Jack Wolfskin* and these boots cost £120,' he boasted, shamelessly.'

'Very impressive, Mr Saul, but if you don't mind me saying, those trousers wouldn't keep a gentle summer shower out, my friend'.

'But they're from *Cotswold*s, you know,' he protested.

Amit looked puzzled. 'That may well be, but where we're heading, we're going to need something far more robust to protect our legs when it starts to snow and the temperature plummets.'

Sarah and Luke had different issues with their equipment. Her flimsy hat and his lack of thermal trousers. They were going to need extra warmth in both places. All of them needed to address issues around keeping their hands warm. Their gloves were not ready for the mountain chills. As Luke was to discover, there are easy ways and hard ways to learn how to dress appropriately in the Himalaya and the hard ways are best left to the folly of the reckless.

Luke had already started learning things the hard way in this country. His decision to sit on the back seat of their Nepalese mini-bus from the airport had left an embarrassing bruise. His damaged *coccyx* might never be the same again.

Meanwhile Sarah and Gurdeep were taking an interest in what Amit was wearing. 'Those pleats in your shirt and the ties, are they some sort of popular or regional fashion'? Sarah enquired.

'Oh no, Miss Sarah, this is not fashion. These are symbols of my Hindu faith. The closed collar represents the snake around Lord Shiva's neck, while the eight pieces to connect the shirt represent the importance of the number eight, a lucky number in both Hinduism and Buddhism'

'I do hope so,' joked Saul. Counting Alan, Amit, Dexa and the five of us, that makes us a party of eight. A good sign, don't you think, Amit?'

Amit grinned and expediently decided not to mention that they also had a ninth person, namely the driver, Sunil.

'What about these pleats?' Gurdeep asked.

'That's another bit of Hindu and Buddhist influence. It represents the *Pancha Ratna* or *Pancha Buddhist* Do you know what they are?'

'I know what *pancha* means, from my Punjabi background, as a Sikh. We also have five marks of identity to remind us of – the five 'K's.'

'Indeed, sister! And whether we're reminding ourselves of the five Hindu *Ratna* songs in praise of Lord Rama, or the five wisdoms of the Buddha, depicted in paintings, within the homes of many Buddhists, they all point towards human needs that we all share.'

'What about the tensions between sharing religious ideas from different faiths?', Gurdeep continued.

'This is Nepal! We learned a long time ago to share our ancient beliefs, rather than compete with one other for them! Our understanding of truth can be strengthened by the acceptance of different images and creeds. They help to open our minds to the acquisition of wisdom. Conflict becomes a barrier to this striving for shared knowledge; this understanding of others.'

Mohammed had joined them and was listening closely. 'Tell me, Amit. Does what you say apply to Muslims, here too?'

'Of course, Mr Mohammed. We have observed from afar the pain of so many Muslim brothers and sisters around the world. So much anger and violence, so much prejudice and discrimination, war and destruction in recent years. But here in our lands, a small number of Islamic families, live their lives, alongside their Nepalese neighbours, in respect and peace'.

Amit's comforting arm reached out to Mohammed. It momentarily lifted a little of the weight that had rested so uneasily upon his tired shoulders in recent weeks. Mohammed stared into Amit's eyes. He thought he detected the faintest glimmer of flame, struggling to emerge. Sufficient embers to light a small fire? A rich metaphor for someone who wanted to grasp the smoulders and ignite so many changes in his own life?

21

A Bumpy Ride

Luke was woken by the raucous sound of large black crows, seemingly competing for the honour of gazing through his bedroom window. He watched them claw and flutter their way along the window sill, jostling for space; like frenzied shoppers, pushing their way through a *Black Friday* sale. Their interest was disconcerting.

He knew he was not at his best this time of the day, especially at 5.00am. Who was? Random thoughts criss-crossed his brain like a lattice of electric pulses. 'Who rises at such an hour?' No one he knew and certainly not him! However, he was in Kathmandu and this was no ordinary day. Luke had a feeling that 23rd November was going to be something of an endurance test. They had been warned about the frustrations of sitting in a clapped -out mini -bus for most of the daylight hours. No wonder, the birds had gathered to gawk. They probably felt sorry for him. With one leg out of bed, he pulled his sweaty fame from the sheets and entered the day. Unfortunately, he hadn't slept that well.

A strong knock on the door reminded Luke it was time to get ready. 'Tea, Sir.' A smiling porter stood there armed with tea-pot and chapatis. Thirty minutes later, Luke was stood in the foyer and ready to embrace what the journey demanded. Well, almost! Looking around, none of them looked particularly energetic. It had been a humid night. Luke was also being summoned by his stomach to adjust his bowel movements, for the third time that morning. It was wise to listen to his body. Playing back seat head rhythms against the roof of the vehicle, was becoming tedious enough. Worrying about the effect of last night's curry was an additional concern he certainly didn't need.

The mini-bus wove its way slowly out of *Thamel*. Past the endless maze of hidden roads, with their numerous shops and hotels, until they turned onto the main route that led out of the city. Most of the others were already asleep again as they joined the multitude of lorries, adorned with their vividly painted religious symbols. The procession of vehicles snaked, slowly along but it had to share the tarmac with others. Nearer the kerbs, cyclists and pedestrians flanked their route, as riders fixing their gaze, inquisitively, when their eyes met with those of the visitors. They were all wisely keeping their distance from these noisy juggernauts that were competing for space with buses, cars, vans and auto rickshaws.

Luke was suddenly distracted by the impact of the latest pot-hole. It jolted him into thinking further. Rubbing the top of his head, he considered what lay in the days ahead. He had managed to glean from Alan that there would be other guests staying with them at his homestead. However, he was evasive about sharing too much information about who these people were.

Eventually the convoy of vehicles started to climb out of the valley in which Kathmandu lay, sprawled out beneath the sprawling smog. The landscape started to change. Neatly tiered terraces of vegetable crops, protected by clusters of banana and coconut trees, decorated the lower hills. The convoy began to move more quickly as the traffic spread out.

Two short stops brought much-needed opportunities to stretch their crumpled legs and eat a little food. However, they were soon back on board again. As the highway continued to rise, snow-capped mountains began to appear in the distance. The road was also beginning to narrow. It started to cling precariously close to the wall of rock that shielded them on the left- hand side. The view from the right was starting to open out in all its splendour. Water-falls could be spotted, carving paths through the rock and forming channels to irrigate the fields, far below. Farmers nurtured the fruit of their labours, as they had done for thousands of years, stacking wheat, rice, vegetables and fruit, in circular barns of bamboo and leaf.

The hours passed slowly. Just when they felt they'd lost the will to absorb another panoramic vista, the mini-bus finally turned off the road and pulled up outside an old wooden building. Luke looked at his watch. It was just before five o'clock.

'We're going to stay here tonight, my friends', Alan bellowed. The collective relief was written across everyone's face. 'Well done! everyone', he continued. 'Not a journey for the feint -hearted, Hey?'

Gurdeep and Sarah made a dash for the toilet, while the fellows leaned against the bus, stretching their necks and limbs back into shape.

Mohammed caught Alan's attention. 'Where are we?'

'We're just outside Pokhara, near the Annapurna massif. Tomorrow we move into the Mars Yangdi river path and onto the gravel road. Then we'll head on up towards Hepsang and my home.'

Amit suggested a pre-dinner walk to blow away the mini-bus cobwebs. They didn't need any persuasion. Even Gurdeep was keen to climb into her boots. While Alan sorted out food arrangements, Amit escorted them up behind the back of the accommodation, to the modest hill, which stood nearby. The late afternoon wind lapped around their faces. It was refreshing to be out in the cool air. With the light starting to fade, they scuttled back down the path, to be met by Alan in the reception area. 'So, I hope that's given you an appetite, everyone. Ready to eat?'

There was no need to ask. Luke and Saul said they were absolutely famished! By ten o clock, they had all retired to their rooms, seeking the comfort of an early night. He may have been sharing a room filled with antiquated bunk- beds, spread-eagled on a solid matrass that felt like concrete, but nothing was going to keep Luke awake for long. Not even Saul's bizarre theories about the new Alan. He dozed off, suspecting that tomorrow would be no easier.

A fan-fare of early morning song from the local cockerels and birds next morning, ensured that none of them enjoyed the lie in they wanted. A combination of lumpy porridge, sweetened with local honey and washed down with strong herbal tea, galvanized the party into action. By 7.30am, they were on the move. The tranquil lake of Phewa Tal, at the edge of Pokhara, appeared in the distance, buttressed on its norther shores by the rising peaks of Annapurna.

'That's my favourite mountain over there. *Machhapuchhre*. We also call it *fishtail*. Can you see why?' Amit pointed to the distinctive shape. They nodded obediently, trying to isolate the source of his gaze. They soon located it from the silhouetted skyline, above the town. One summit flanked by the pinnacles of so many others.

Alan announced that they would be spending a couple of days there at the end of the trip, enjoying the delights of Nepal's second most famous urban community. Within an hour and a half, the mini-bus had taken them across to Besi Shahar and the start of the classic Annapurna trekking route. The small town was a hive of activity, as groups of international walkers assembled outside hotels and guest houses to begin their journey on foot. They could see pathways cut into the side of the mountains and below, a dusty gravel road of sorts, churning up pillars of dust with each lorry that went past. They joined them, bumping along, holding on to the rims of their seats. Despite the heat, the windows remained shut to protect them from the dust. Unfortunately, the air-conditioning system had reached that stage of its life when even an intermittent trickle of cool air was a bonus.

Their road had been blasted through with explosives; hewed from the lower slopes of the mountain. It was barely passable for a vehicle like theirs, which had certainly seen better days. Looking ahead, they could see how the route followed the twisting pattern of the waters below.

The river basin began to widen, revealing a huge expanse of flat, dried stones and pebbles. The flowing water occupied a fraction of the whole riverbed. Enormous tree trunks, pulled from the mountain side by ferocious storms, stacked up against rocks, boulders and other debris that the violent weather conditions had torn from the ground. In the silence of pre-winter, they could only imagine the power and fear that this river would generate when swollen by seasonal storms and floods.

They passed several small villages, which were propped up, precariously, above the river's edge. The rock faces now grew taller and more foreboding. Annapurna 11 and IV appeared before them, crowned by ice and snow in the upper reaches of their 7-8,000 metre pinnacles.

Eventually, they came to a halt. To be more precise, it was the road that had come to a halt.

'Okay, everyone. From here on in, we walk,' Alan instructed the group. In front of them lay a track, lined by bamboo trees and meandering up to a pine forest. 'We need to climb up through the woods', Alan explained. 'Then we head over the suspension bridge and cross the ridge, over there. Peering above the tree -line was a jagged outcrop of dark rock. Beyond that hill, we'll descend into my valley and our destination.' There was discernible pride in the tone of his voice. They looked at each other, trying to work out how long it was going to take. It was already two in the afternoon.

The walking was not easy. Many of the paths they trod now were narrow and treacherous. Several local men suddenly appeared, carrying familiar looking large kitbags. Their bags!

They nonchalantly eased past them and disappeared into the trees. By the time, they'd reached the woods, another hour had gone by.

Their route took them through a thicket of enormous pine trees; their copious branches, sheltering them from the brightness of the light. Only the faded buds of late summer's rhododendron plants brought a touch of colour to the ground.

'What's that smell,'? Saul suddenly shouted out as they approached a thicket of deep, green plants.

Luke recognised the pungent scent immediately and smiled knowingly at Saul. 'I think I recognise it', he said. 'What does our resident scientist think,'? he said, provocatively, turning to Gurdeep.

'I think you guys know exactly what that is!', she retorted, with the consternation of a police officer.

The two men laughed and were joined by Alan.

'There's more cannabis here than anyone could consume,' he exclaimed. 'And it grows out in the wild, just like here.'

Twenty minutes later, they stood in front of a one hundred metre drop. The cliff-face gave way to a vertical chasm, which met the river below. 'Don't worry, my friends. This bridge is quite safe. Made of steel. Not like that one over there.' Alan pointed to what was left of a decrepit looking wooden bridge, close by, held together with rope lashed around the beams. Several pieces were missing, presumably having plunged into the river.   Muhammed strode forward confidently.

'Come on. I'm sure Alan's right. Let's go!'

The party carefully crossed the steel bridge, trying not to peer down at the river below. Gurdeep was grateful for the supportive arm, offered by Amit. The others managed to negotiate their way across the swaying steel construction, confident, that the metal supports would do their job.

The final ascent was mercifully short. Within thirty minutes, they were standing at the top of the dark ridge, staring down at Alan's farm. Their refuge in the valley. Across from the buildings stood timeless mountain terrains. These highest peaks were decorated with significant falls of snow. Another river meandered away into the distance, across the valley floor. It was a breath-taking sight.

Their spirits started to lift with each descending step they took, as they dragged their tired limbs down the final path to their destination. The sun was starting to fade from the sky, as an emerging wind chilled their faces. They walked, wearily, towards the collection of buildings in front of them.

'Welcome, my friends, to my home. My 'Shangri La!' A large, three-tiered building stood before them. Two excited women came out to greet them, insisting on taking their day-sacks. They were grateful to lose them. The walk from the mini-bus had taken over three hours and their shoulders ached.

'These ladies are Eaimar and Karuna. They will be looking after you during your stay here for the next few days,' Alan announced. 'Please, come inside. I guess you've had enough fresh air for one afternoon'

They gingerly limped through the door to find Dexa and Amit preparing a fire at the end of the room. Luke's attention was drawn to an impressive oval table, placed in the centre of the room, surrounded by a dozen hard-backed chairs. Brightly coloured mats lay on the seats and backs of the chairs to add some comfort. To the right, a large, imposing statue of the Buddha lay in reclining mode. The flaking plaster looked quite old. Much of the gold -leaf that once adorned its exterior had faded away. Above them, connected by a wooden stairway, was a network of small rooms. These extended across and around the room below, mirroring the rectangular shape of the building. Another set of stairs led to a third level of rooms.

The house looked robust and just about everything seemed to be built from hardwood. Several oak beams lay across the ceiling, securing the dining room roof and supporting the higher floors above them. It looked like a property constructed to stand firm against anything nature could throw at it. Luke was sure he wasn't alone in thinking about the enormity of the challenge, in securing the construction of such buildings, in such a desolate place. He looked through the window, across the foothills and towards the shadow of the mighty Annapurna circuit. It seemed unnervingly close to them.

22

Samixya

That evening it started to snow. At first, quite gently, but later in the night, the sky was lit up with a myriad of snowflakes. Not that any of them noticed. Sturdy beds with warm quilts, lined with the insulation of yak hair, had nullified the aches and pains of the journey.

When they awoke, the following day, the fields and hills were covered in a carpet of white. Like a Christmas card cover, Luke said to his room-mate, except for the towering mountains. 'Hardly Judea!' Saul added, with a pedantic sigh.

Luke descended the squeaky steps which led down to the eating area. Sarah and Muhammed were already standing outside the front door, admiring the pristine morning view. It wasn't early. Alan had promised them a lie-in after their journey and he was true to his word. Breakfast had been delayed until nine.

'Morning, you two!' He extended an enthusiastic greeting to his colleagues.

'Just look at that view, Luke', Sarah replied. 'I can't believe we're actually here!'

He nodded. As they consumed the food in front of them, everybody admitted that they'd slept well.

After breakfast, Alan offered to show them around the complex. There was much more to his home-stead than they had seen when they arrived. Behind the building in which they had slept and eaten in, lay two smaller constructions. They looked like living quarters. Next to them was some sort of barn. Inside, two small yaks were munching their way through a trough of mixed vegetables, while chickens wandered aimlessly through the yard. Luke watched their eyes, eagerly hunting, surreptitiously, for any loose seeds that had been spilled on the ground.

Alan pointed out ed the two smaller houses on the right where Dexa and Amit lived. They were, he added, a central part of *Sanctuary*. They looked up. The name of the homestead was carved on a wooden plaque, outside the main building.

The party came to the perimeter gate and carried on, across the field. The overpowering smell of animal dung, ambushed Luke's nostrils as he walked passed an old shed. They all quickened their pace and turned the corner to face the breeze. Alan had anticipated their reactions.

'Yes. Yak dung can take some getting used to. But its oh, so vital here! In many of the valleys communities use it for fuel as well as for fertilizer. Really rich in nutrients.' He continued. 'I want to show you all something. Up there, below that ridge, is a very special place. It will only take us about twenty minutes.'

Sarah and Gurdeep looked at each other, lamenting this unexpected extension to their morning stroll. The porridge was still settling in their stomachs. However, they pulled up their hoods, against the wind, fastened up their coats and followed Alan and the others out of the compound.

As they moved nearer to the ridge, the outline of a Buddhist *stupa* or tower appeared, out of the mist. Multi-coloured prayer flags were festooned around the perimeter of a small, stone-clad shrine. They climbed the chiselled steps which led to the entrance and found themselves outside a small cave. The scent of sandalwood filled the air, driven by clusters of glowing joss sticks. The air felt colder here as the mists hovered just above them. It helped to create an atmosphere, pregnant with expectation. Alan stood next to the heavy curtain, which hung across the entrance and spoke to them.

'I want you all to meet someone. Her name is Samixya. She is a Buddhist monk and lives here. Can I ask you to go inside individually, to receive a blessing from her? Just greet Samixya with a respectful bow. A few rupees would be a kind gesture. And just to let you know, she doesn't speak any English.'

Luke can still remember the look she gave him when he entered the cave. There was something disconcerting about this frail old lady stretching out an emaciated hand over his head and whispering unknown words from a forgotten age. Almost like an act of anointment, he thought. As if reading his sense of unease, she croaked a familiar *Namaste* and smiled, benignly. He was transfixed by her serenity.

Descending the steps, the group was noticeably quiet, even subdued. Luke was pre-occupied with thoughts about the elderly woman. Here was a woman who must have been in her middle 80's. How did she survive in such an exposed outcrop of mountain rock? Why would someone choose to live like this? Did she not have any family members to look after her?

As they reached the house, the rich aroma of coffee wafted, invitingly, towards them. Everybody migrated towards the dining area and this time Amit and Dexa joined them. Alan was keen to gauge their impressions from the walk. Sipping his drink, he nonchalantly threw out a vague question in the direction of their assembled faces. 'So, what do you think about my little slice of heaven here, then?'

Gurdeep was the first to respond. She spoke about the sense of strength and contentment she felt, being in the presence of a woman like Samixya. Sarah agreed and found the simple act of receiving a blessing from the monk, profoundly moving. Mohammed expressed his surprise that such an elderly woman could endure such spartan living conditions, while Saul and Luke wondered about her welfare and safety, up on the ridge. As they shared their observations, Dexa and Amit listened attentively.

Eventually, Dexa, in a clear English accent, addressed them: 'My friends, these comments are all very interesting. Do you not think it raises some questions about our own lives and what we consider to be important?'

The profound nature of the question could not be ignored. Mohammed was clearly keen to explore the subject further. His contrast between what they would identify as essentials in their lives and what Samixya seemed to need, helped to sharpen their reflections. Alan said it would prove an interesting exercise for each of them to list the things they would miss the most, if drawn to live a similar monastic lifestyle. Saul was brutally honest and admitted he could never entertain the notion. 'My list would require several sheets of A4!'

Gurdeep pointed out that she could empathise with the Buddhist monk. She had been brought up with similar traditions in India. Wandering *sadhu*, holy men, were common sights amongst the temples and forests of the sub-continent. She remarked that there was something about the stillness and solitude of the cave that must help Samixya to discard all those distractions of the mind. The things which bombarded people like them, constantly throughout the day. Surely, this must aid the mind to focus with greater discipline and clarity.

Dexa intensified her studious gaze and prompted further comments around the potential benefits of such isolation. 'So, tell me, my friends, how do you free your minds from the clutter of daily life? In that moment, Luke remembered Alan's comment about the meaning of Dexa's name: '*to teach*'. Luke could see where this discussion was heading. Here was a skilled educator at work.

When she asked them to name one thing they believed they would find hard to live without, the answers came in thick and fast. They were illuminating; a dependency on alcohol, attitudes to women, the need for hope, transparency, honesty and security, emerged at random. Alan and his Nepalese friends threw some alternative ideas into the melting -pot: conscientiousness, loving kindness and self -discipline. These were very different essentials. It created a mixed concoction of human traits, weaknesses and values to peruse. Luke sensed that this discussion was about to open a can of worms. It did.

Saul, rather clumsily, attempted to summarize what he thought these ideas had in common, but gave way to Dexa's intervention. 'I want you all to find some space in the complex, to reflect more on this. Please do so in a location of solitude. Let the mind breathe, without the distractions of others, for one hour. Then, we will talk again about this tomorrow.'

Slowly, each one of them slid away to find a place of solitude and reflect more deeply about the things they most valued in their lives; the things people often cling on to. Luke decided to put his coat on and venture outside. The frosty air normally aided his concentration.

They were all much quieter at dinner, that evening. The events of the day had begun to slow down the anxieties they had brought with them about the trip. However, they were starting to raise new, more profound questions about themselves. 'Sanctuary' was starting to live up to its name! Despite the fears and concerns they had carried, along with their ruck-sacks, everyone was starting to feel more at home in Hepsang.

The following morning saw everyone up early, refreshed and eager. Alan had arranged another walk for them, after breakfast, but this time they'd been asked to avoid speaking to each other on the trail. 'Just use your senses. Focus on what you can see, touch, feel, smell and hear. We'll go out, stay together, so no one gets lost, and climb a little higher than yesterday.'

The party set out as the sunlight broke through thick, bilious clouds, which had gathered before day-break. Luke thought that every feature of the landscape had been lit up in golden streaks of yellow, as if crafted by the hand of an artist. It bathed the terrain in a sharp, luminous glow.

They found it difficult not to talk to each other. A discipline Luke had already found uncomfortable. Best to walk several paces apart. *Don't invite distraction*, he mused. Especially from Saul! They headed off, through the fields, but away from the ridge where Samixya was no doubt, performing her daily rituals. This time, they moved towards the formidable mountains on their left. It wasn't long before they reached the snow-line. Walking through the snow and slush was precarious and began to slow them down but they applied their walking poles to the task of steadying their balance. They trekked on. There was no hurry. What they didn't realise was that there was no specific destination! The act of walking in isolation, alone with their thoughts, was going to be sufficient for this planned exercise. It would concentrate their minds; help to open their senses to the whole, holistic experience of just being there. Luke tried to absorb everything he could. Not surprisingly, his eyes were already saturated with what he had absorbed. He became aware of distant birds, guarding the high canyons above, weaving ever-changing patterns on the winds. Maybe, they were watching him. Like predators, preparing to feast on his carcass, should he stumble, and his life expire. Normally, he would have shared the humour with Saul, but he was out of reach, alone with his own considerations.

With each second that passed, Luke's other senses became more alive to the environment around him. The intermittent sound of cracking, as boots penetrated pockets of ice, brought a sharp contrast to the gentle, monotonous rhythm of pale, crusted, snowy footsteps. The touch of a freshly released hand upon the rock, numbing the fingers and imploring the brain to demand an immediate retreat, back to the security of a warm glove. The taste of freshly fallen snow, tingling on the edge of one's tongue, invigorating the mouth. Even the plucking of an occasional leaf from the pole's spike, left trapped in nature's graveyard, brought back faded smells of yesteryear. They reminded his nostrils of what lay below winter's blanket of decay.

All of this and more came pouring out, as they sat together at the table, three hours later. Dexa had a question for the group to consider: could they describe what they noticed out there, today? This released an energy in Luke that was both surprising and uncomfortable. There was so much to process in his head.

'It's good to bare your soul, occasionally', Sarah suddenly exclaimed.

'Articulate those feelings. I don't know about the rest of you, but these days, I don't seem to get many opportunities like this to do it.'

Later, after supper, they talked again. This time Amit led the discussion. 'Some aspects of what we did and saw today, must have seemed quite strange to you, my friends. You might have been thinking: how can people be so content with what seems to be, so little? In many societies, there are people who define others by what they own, rather than who they are. An obsession with the external, rather than the internal person. Many Westerners I have met, seem pre-occupied with how much they earn or how valuable their homes and possessions are. The same is true in our Asian cities. It appears to me that the more they obtain, the more they desire and want. The hunger for more never dies. There is something profoundly significant about this endless pursuit of wealth. A restlessness, born of insecurity. Clearly, owning more than we need does not bring lasting happiness. When we reflect upon the human misery that results from selfishness, we understand that a desire for purpose and inner peace will only come from the generosity of giving. So why is this?

'Could it be that people are looking in the wrong place for answers to these questions? Should we not invest more time attempting to discover greater meaning in our lives? Indulgence and greed have fuelled a sub-culture of physical and mental deterioration. Such people seem to be falling into an ever-deepening abyss, where loneliness, illness and despair have blighted their lives. That is why I believe that this modern world, with all its advantages and technological advances, needs to find more space for reflection and contemplation. We need to recognise that the human spirit still requires opportunities to develop; to reach out for spiritual growth.'

There were several furrowed brows around the table, reflecting on what they had heard. Saul distracted Luke with one of those cynical expressions he often displayed, when he was uncomfortable about something. This was followed by him silently miming the word spiritual to his friend, with a quizzical expression. Luke knew what he meant. It wasn't his thing. It occurred to him that maybe Saul was still hiding from the person he might become. If only he could cut through all those distractions.

Sarah interrupted Luke's train of thought by suddenly sharing with the rest of them, a memory from her school days. It concerned puberty and her teenage dreams. Saul's concentration levels quickened! Sarah could see herself back in church; an awkward adolescent dragooned into attending a school penitential service. Struggling to articulate her transgressions before 'God's representative', the priest. In those days, her sins were largely imaginings about the vanity of personal beauty or acts of romantic intimacy with 'fit' boys. Oh, the excitement of sexual awakening! However, her parents cautioned her with different words. Self-respect, modesty, disgust and shame, were raised to reinforce the undoubted dangers associated with getting too close to boys (any suggestion of same-sex partners would have sent them spinning into homophobic meltdown!) Curiously, she remembered an unhelpful pre-occupation with that much maligned biblical character Mary Magdalene and her dubious profession.

Sarah had long concluded that the patchy details that emerged from such New Testament figures, rendered any relevant link to her life pointless. In fact, Sarah had always viewed Jesus's closest female friend, sympathetically. A strong female character in a world of powerful men. Her relationship with the carpenter from Nazareth, she thought, was a thing of beauty. The absence of strong female figures in the story of Jesus was noticeable. In Sarah's view, Mary was not tarnished because of her dubious reputation. If she had facilitated the sexual needs of men, then so what? After all, these were guys who hoped their shadowy activities might disguise the hypocrisy of their actions. When it came to prostitution, she concluded, nothing seemed to have changed over the centuries.

They soon learned where this anecdote was heading. She had identified a real barrier to her own transformation, long ago and it had a name. It had nothing to do with sex. Sarah declared that her dependency on alcohol was at the root of most of her problems and transgressions. In her own mind, it was impossible to deny. This was not a revelation to the rest of them. She had always drunk a lot and didn't disguise the fact.

Was the comfort of regular intoxication creating her abyss, she said, sheltering her from the isolation of loneliness? How honest had she been with herself in the past, when faced with the pressures and disappointments of life?

Luke listened, transfixed, as he always used to, when Sarah bared her soul. He felt the urge to say something about himself. Something to distract her from the outpourings of her testament. Words slowly emerged. 'Sarah, I also struggle with a challenge. No, struggle is the wrong word: I don't struggle with it, I run away! It scares me. My transgressions are drawn from the panic of inertia, apathy. What I need to ask myself is: How do I find the courage to step outside my comfort zone? Face up to my lack of drive; my fear of change. Yes, there have been traumas in my life, but who hasn't faced situations which were difficult?' Luke told them he preferred to seek comfort behind closed walls. Things were too cosy to take chances. His weaknesses, his sins were lethargy and apathy. He was simply not prepared to put himself out. Take a risk; explore who he might become.

He needed to stop trying to avoid fundamental issues about his future; let alone the wider philosophical questions about life and death. He knew he would be seized by a sense of panic if he ever seriously addressed the question of how he might, as a person, need to change. Luke sat back in his chair, temporarily paralysed by his excruciatingly act of personal character assassination. Like Sarah, it had felt like a confession. In those moments, he knew a weight had been lifted.

Mohammed shuffled awkwardly, before enticing the attention of those assembled. He cleared of his throat and spoke up. 'Thanks for your honesty, Luke. You're not alone on this one. Much of what you say about the fear of change and facing up to who you really are, is a feature of my weakness, too. Back in those days when we were students, you guys helped me to grow up. You may not have intended to bring this about, but you challenged me about my faith in a way that others inside my circle of friends and family did not. Like many other young adherents of religion, I was drunk with optimism in those days. God was going to look after me; protect me, even if I didn't know exactly how but all those jokes, the lampooning, the challenging of my ideas, forced me to reflect more critically about my beliefs; particularly about one, specific moral issue. It also, indirectly, began a process. One that has only recently come to a head in my life. It enabled me to realise something that I've always known, but never been able to admit. At least, not publicly, not until recently'.

The atmosphere was palpable. Even Alan, had suspended his tranquil demeanour, in the expectation that he was about to hear something crucial. Mohammed fixed his gaze, intrigued with what seemed to be leading to some sort of imminent declaration. 'You see, what I hidden from all of you, and even from my wife and relatives, over many years, is that…I'm gay.'

There are moments when any combination of words a person might choose to muster, will fail, miserably to encapsulate the significance of an announcement. Easier to retreat into silence. Better still, let your actions speak for you. While most of them fumbled with surprise, Gurdeep stood up and walked over to Mohammed. She threw her arms around him. 'That must be the bravest things you've ever done, Mohammed. Carrying this secret around, for all this time, must have been such a burden. My heart goes out to you'.

It provoked a response from the rest of them. In between vacuous murmurs of approval from Saul and Luke, Sarah joined Gurdeep in embracing Mohammed.

Meanwhile, Dexa and Amit, were busy assembling their own homily of support, while Alan having regained his tranquil smile, clasped his hands together in an act of respect, towards Mo.

Dexa clapped her hands, reinforcing the general feeling of support. She sat back in her chair and looked up to the ceiling, as if summoning pictures from her past. 'I feel privileged to hear the heartfelt witness of those gathered here. It seems like there has been an out-pouring of such honesty circling the room, that the therapeutic impact has touched each of us, profoundly. I am also sure that we can all absorb the trust they have placed in our hands and support our companions. I would like to add to it now by sharing something of my own story.

'I too carry a burden that reminds me of something every day of my life; that we are sometimes challenged to choose difficult paths in life. Many years ago, I lived on the other side of the Himalaya, in Tibet. Life was good. I had a devoted husband and two young boys. I worked there as a teacher at the local school and loved my job. Then, one Saturday in June, the Chinese soldiers arrived. They were looking for some of the villagers. I was on their list. I still don't know why. I remember being struck with batons when I protested, as they pushed me into the lorry. I lost consciousness. The last thing I saw was the anguished looks on the

103

face of my husband and children as their mother was driven away. When I woke up, I was lying in a gloomy prison cell. It smelt of damp and human excrement. All I could hear were the cries of the incarcerated.

'The guards visited me each day. They hurt me. They laughed when I pleaded for mercy. I became a broken vessel. The only thing I looked forward to, was death. Then, there was a fire one night at the prison camp. Amidst the smoke and confusion, some of us managed to escape. We had to make a choice. Turn north, towards the village and almost certain re-capture, or south across the Himalayan paths towards the freedom of Nepal. That was five years ago. I haven't seen or heard from my family since.

'You may be wondering how I came to be here, at Alan's place. He found me in a refugee camp near the border. We became friends. When he told me of his plans, I was delighted to join him, at his *Sanctuary* up here in the Nepalese mountains.' She paused for a few seconds, searching for the words to continue. 'Not a day goes by when I don't feel the anguish of that decision. Who knows what has become of my family. All I do know is that my heart broke into a thousand pieces the day I lost sight of them.'

The was not so much as a murmur in the room. Amit placed his hand on top of Dexa's. Luke couldn't have been the only one struggling to imagine what a living nightmare this must be for her. Nor, how incompatible, some of their so-called burdens must have seemed.

Gurdeep's glance suggested that she had read his thoughts and she began to speak to the group. 'Listening to Dexa's story, with the tragic loss of her family, makes me realise how some people are destined to carry much greater loads than others. I think the important thing for us is to try and take something positive, even inspirational, from Dexa's testimony. We cannot change what happened, but I think there are aspects of it which can help us with the tests that come our way. She has had to bear this sadness, every single day of her life since. Yet, we would not have known this, if she hadn't had the courage to share these details with us, today. I think her dignity and grace must be born of some colossal inner strength. To accept such circumstances, which, if she was to survive, could not be avoided, nor changed. Looking back, I know that the hand of fate can deal all of us situations which quickly become cloaked in pain. Sometimes, they change your life. It did for me.

'When I was a student, I erected tall fences defences around me. You saw only a guarded face. Gurdeep the industrious, the dedicated, the studious. That was only part of me! I realised I wasn't very successful in hiding my sadness. At least you left me alone. I thank you for doing so. I really wasn't ready to tell you, then. But I'm ready to tell you now.'

Gurdeep described how she changed from a lively, innocent, intelligent girl, into a broken young woman, struggling to find the will to carry on. Her mother's sadness; the insensitivity of her father; the cruelty of her brothers and the brutal assaults by her husband that characterised her marriage, were poured out to her incredulous companions. The experience had scarred her; building a frigidity within, that would prevent the possibility of intimacy with another man in the future. That trust was no longer there. She was keen to emphasise that she could now see that there had also been moments of hope and acts of great kindness in this episode. The sympathy and guile of her aunt, the compassion of an elderly cart driver, the generosity of a shopkeeper's family in Amritsar. There was also her protection of a passport forger there, against the unwanted sexual attention of his boss, who desired more than just money from her, in payment for the document. Finally, the support of a British Sikh family, who had be-friended her when she first arrived in the UK. They had all contributed to her survival.

Her face looked relaxed and conveyed the relief of a burden, finally lifted.

Amidst all this harrowing reflection and shared grief, Saul sat quietly. Luke ribbed him, as they retired for bed, that night.

'Can't wait for Saul Cohen's story. Is that one coming tomorrow?', he muttered, provocatively.

Saul looked at him and grimaced. 'When I feel I'm ready', came his curt reply.

23

Familiar tales in Hepsang

The following morning, a misty, grey Saturday, had been ear-marked by Alan for his guests to visit a local village. The wind had died down and there had been no further snowfall. He wanted them to meet some of the people he had befriended and thought it would be good for them to learn a little about how his neighbours lived. He had chosen them, carefully. After breakfast, they all assembled in the hallway. Gurdeep and Sarah were missing. Sarah eventually appeared, to explain that her roommate had been sick in the night and was complaining of headaches.

'Okay. Tell her to stay here and we'll catch up with her later. Dexa will look after her,' Alan announced.

The rest of them set off, with Alan and Amit, to amble the one and a half kilometres to Lower Hepsang, in the valley below. Half an hour later, they were standing at the arched gate which marked the beginning of the village territory and Saul was studying the stone construction with interest.

'Amit. These images attached to the pillar; the figures contained inside the glass panes. Are they some sort of demons; there to protect the community from their enemies? This one, looks like that *Mara* figure back in the hotel at Kathmandu'

Amit moved closer to peruse the artefacts and pictures. 'No, my friend. These are Hindu deities, images of God, to help and inspire people. Look! This one is *Ganesh*, bringer of luck and good fortune. A very popular deity! Your Mara is more likely to be found on the other pillar, Saul. This is where the Buddhist images are placed.'

Luke smiled and walked across with Saul to inspect the second column of stones. These two pillars were connected at the top by a huge wooded beam, with more brightly coloured artefacts decorating the length of the plinth.

Amit interrupted them. 'The thing is, Saul, these images lie next to each other for a reason. They emphasise the importance of tolerance and respect among Buddhists and Hindus. There is little religious conflict here. Local people understand that it is better to meet the challenges of life alongside your neighbour, rather than be in conflict with them.'

Standing back a few paces to take a photo of the group, Saul was struck by the way the entrance gate had framed the buildings of the village behind it, like a picture postcard. It seemed to encapsulate a tiny fragment of Himalayan life. He wondered what the inhabitants made of these curious foreigners strolling into their world. By doing so, did they become part of their story now too?

They walked slowly down the path into Hepsang. Alan continued: 'I would ask you to be cautious, my friends, as we enter the village. Some of the locals are still suspicious of outsiders and may come across as a little reticent'.

As if to reinforce the point, an elderly woman appeared from her house and stood, transfixed, by their arrival. She stared intensely at Luke, walked across in front of him and began to urinate on the floor. He wasn't sure how he was supposed to respond to something like this.

'Don't worry, Luke', Alan called across to him. 'You probably caught her by surprise. Some aspects of life continue, regardless of who walks through the village.'

A group of noisy teenage boys offered a timely distraction. They were clustered together, with sticks, manoeuvring something on the ground. They eventually caught sight of their prey. A small, green snake was thrashing around aimlessly in the dust. Its head lay severed, at the side.

'Welcome to Hepsang!'

They carried on walking, past ramshackle huts of wood and stone, enmeshed with corrugated sheets of plastic. Simple stockades had been constructed of twisted sticks and wire. They surrounded the houses, providing enclosures for the chickens, cockerels and other animals that lived there. More elderly inhabitants started to appear. Some peered through faded curtains, while others sat outside on the steps which had been freshly chalked in patterns of yellow, green, gold and red powder. These men and women had friendlier faces, which lit up with wide smiles, as the visitors passed by them. Orange flowers lay festooned around many of the doorways and the re-assuring sound of laughter could be heard within.

'It's the feast of Diwali', Amit announced. 'Today is brother and sister day, when family members give each other presents.' It certainly explained why so many of the children were holding hands, instead of teasing each other, as children often do.

They kept on walking and eventually came to a restaurant building, reassuringly called the 'Happy Eating House.' Appetites had been stoked by their efforts and they were ready for lunch. Several people had already gathered at the place and they all appeared to know Alan and Amit. The introductions took several minutes as each of the strangers was introduced to the group. Saul and Luke did their best to remember each name as individuals offered their welcomes.

Alan and Amit escorted the western guests to specific places around the large table that had been set out before them. Luke noticed that each of their party had one of the local villagers sat next to them. It surprised him that they all seemed able to speak, at least a little English. Seated alongside Luke was a large, jolly looking man, with pronounced rosy cheeks, called Channa. Luke found it difficult not to stare at the absence of his left arm. He brought up the subject as they started to eat. Channa told Luke he had lost it in an accident in the mountains, while looking for some of his goats. They had strayed on to an overhanging mountain ledge and didn't seem able to climb back to safety. He had done what any shepherd would do, in these circumstances. 'But, with my extra weight', he continued, 'the whole ledge collapsed, taking me and the goats with it', he casually informed him. 'I was lucky to survive. Two of my goats endured the fall and lived to bear youngsters', he smiled. 'That helped me to bear my pain, knowing the creatures had not perished. Others were not so lucky. I found it difficult to manage such activities afterwards, so I took up a new line of work.'

Amit appeared, hovering with a tray of drinks. 'What he probably didn't tell you was that he crawled half-way down that mountain with one arm so badly crushed that the medical centre immediately severed the limb, or he would have bled to death. He still hadn't abandoned his goats. One injured youngster was nestling under his coat, when some neighbouring farmers found him, prostrate, at the edge of the lower slopes.'

Channa raised his head and said, 'It had to be done. He would have frozen to death, in those temperatures'.

Luke was struck by the man's story. He found his tenacity and determination to survive, deeply moving. But his positive outlook was really what impressed him. Take stock. Adjust. Be positive. Move on, he said to himself. Keep believing there is hope. How would he have dealt with such a traumatic event? Quite differently, he was sure. Frankly, he would never had coped with the challenge for he knew his own fundamental weakness. Luke's dissatisfaction with his life; his inertia and despondency about the problems he faced, loomed, like an unavoidable reflection from an ancient mirror. It presented him with an interesting dilemma.

Channa bent down, picked up an old case made from animal skins, and lifted a picture from it. 'This is what I do now,' he said. A stunning painting of the surrounding peaks and valleys was placed upon Luke's lap. 'Here, accept it as a gift, to remind you of your visit.'

Luke struggled for the words to respond. Instead, he resolved, that day, to try and see the world with a little more of Channa's tenacity of spirit.

Meanwhile, Sarah had started to talk to the man, sat on her right-hand side. From the look of him, he would normally be the sort of stranger she would give a wide birth to. Gaunt, emaciated, with dark folds of skin stacked beneath his eyes, hair dishevelled and prematurely grey, he carried the sort of demeanour that told a troubled story. She wasn't sure it was one she wanted to here. This looked like a man who understood the meaning of hard times. In the name of good manners, she nervously began to engage him in conversation and was astonished to learn that he used to be a regional administrator, with responsibility for over a hundred employees.

As the details of his story unfolded, she became more intrigued. Married with three children, life had once been good for him. That was, until he started to drink. It began innocuously, with occasional beers after work, but this soon degenerated into bouts of heavy alcohol consumption. He widened his drinking tastes to include spirits and rice wine and started to bring bottles into work. He would disappear at every opportunity to imbibe. Toilets, cupboards, the safety of his vehicle; they all provided the necessary cover to hide his addiction from critical eyes. It was only a matter of time before he made a serious misjudgement. In his case, it involved a fatal car crash. He was the driver. He'd taken that bend in the road many times before. But on that day, his judgement was impaired. In those vital seconds when he needed to swerve away from the on-coming vehicle, his reactions were too slow. He still had the half- empty bottle of rice wine in his jacket. His victim was a father of two. Killed on his way home to celebrate his son's birthday.

The enquiry, like his inebriation, was damning. Losing his job was the start of a downward trend, leading to the brink of self -destruction. He became estranged from his family and the villagers who had once respected him. Amit found him one day, lying at the roadside. He thought the prostrate figure, lying in front of him was dead. This shadow of a man, his confidence shattered and hope vanishing with every drink, wished he was dead. But Amit brought him back to his homestead and helped him find a reason to carry on living. His self-respect had begun to return, and he had recently been reconciled with his wife and children. Now he hoped to find work with Alan and one day, earn forgiveness from the family of the man he had killed through his drunken driving. He hadn't had an alcoholic drink for more than six months.

Sarah realised that this encounter was too much of a coincidence to be un-planned. She looked across at Alan and Amit and pondered. It was not by accident that she had been sat next to this man. But it was a story she needed to hear. Sarah hadn't told anyone about the other reason she had left her former career behind, so abruptly. It wasn't just the political correctness or the bureaucracy. The disciplinary hearing had had a major bearing too. Caught driving under the influence of alcohol. Just like her companion. An experienced social worker, transporting a vulnerable mother and child to a safe-guarding meeting. Stopped by the police for erratic driving. Breathalysed. Over the limit, and it was barely one o' clock in the afternoon. A story that the local paper was only too happy to circulate to their outraged readers.

Whenever she felt low, or under pressure, alcohol was still her first port of call. She knew it couldn't continue like this. It was gradually destroying her. There had also been previous warnings from her line -manager. Even the loss of her career hadn't brought it under control. There had to be a way of dealing with this.

To their surprise, Gurdeep suddenly appeared, mounted on the back seat of a rickety old cart. Luke thought it a comical sight, as she perched on the top of a bale of straw. The cart was drawn by a powerful looking horse, adorned with vivid black and white patches across its body. An attractive beast. Next to Gurdeep Dexa crouched, controlling the reins. 'I was feeling much better, so I asked Dexa to bring me over to the restaurant. Hope that is ok', Gurdeep called across, to the party.

'You're just in time, Gurdeep', Alan replied. 'Hope you've found your appetite again. The chick-pea curry is delicious!'

She climbed down and made her way to the extended table at which they were all sitting.

'No! Not there,' Alan responded. 'Please come and sit here. There is someone I'd like you to meet.'

Gurdeep was guided to a seat next to an attractive, statuesque woman, draped in a beautifully embroidered green and white sari. 'Hello Gurdeep', she said. 'My name is Heena. I gather, you were not feeling well, earlier.'

Gurdeep exchanged pleasantries and re-assured her that her headaches were probably just a touch of mountain sickness.

'Yes, quite possibly', her companion replied.' It takes time to adjust to the altitude.'

Gurdeep was drawn to the large piece of jewellery, encrusted with a single stone, on Heena's left hand. 'I love your ring.'

'A gift from my betrothed', Heena responded, with noticeable pride. 'We are to be married in the spring. I never thought this would happen to me, again. The gods have smiled upon me; showered me with many blessings'

'You said *again*. Do I deduce you were married before, Heena?'

The woman nodded, but her expression changed. She recounted how her father had arranged a marriage to a local farmer, many years ago, but it had turned into a living nightmare. She still carried the scars. 'He used to beat me', she confessed. 'I didn't know what to do. I felt so helpless. Mercifully, there were no children. My release from this torment finally came when he was killed in a fight, two years ago. But now my suffering has been transformed by the appearance in my life of a new partner. Trusting another man has not been easy. But he is everything my former husband was not. Kind, thoughtful and sensitive. Tell me, Gurdeep, are you married?'

Although Gurdeep had been listening to Heena, her mind had transported her elsewhere. She was back in the Punjab, all those years ago, with her own marital nightmare. She could see him there: Manreet, sneering menacingly over her, ready to abuse her again. There was her mother too, standing, head bowed, with that look of resignation she often carried. The thought of it still enraged Gurdeep. 'Stand up to him' is what she wanted her mother to say. But Survinder couldn't. The image of her father, Amadeep, was there too, hovering, like an irrepressible beast. She shuddered. It was as if the two women had been living in parallel worlds, hundreds of miles apart. Gurdeep had developed that taste in her mouth again; the one she always got, when the subject of her marriage came up.

She finally gave Heena an answer to her question. 'Yes, I was, but I walked away from that life a long time ago.' Her normal guardedness dissolved as Gurdeep shared the details of her early life and relationship with Manreet. The trauma, the frustrations, the loss of her family, all tumbled out. The other woman listened to her with a shared empathy.

'Don't let this destroy you, Gurdeep. I once felt the same way. There are other men out there, who have the capacity to love and cherish you. They are not all like Manreet. Do not abandon the idea of finding such affection with another. Otherwise, your former husband will have succeeded, in damaging your heart. He will have destroyed your spirit; your sense of hope. You deserve better. Just like me and the countless thousands of sisters around the world who are witnesses to their own life of abuse.'

Heena's words resonated with the woman from Northern India.

Luke, meanwhile, looked across to see where his friend Saul was seated. He located him at the end of the table. He couldn't but notice the young man sitting next to him. He looked tall and strikingly handsome. Not dissimilar to Saul. That was, until his flamboyant gesticulations revealed the other side of his face. Previously hidden by strands of thick, black hair, his right cheek and neck were now exposed. His features revealed a different image. Deep scars lacerated his cheek. Around them, several swollen red blotches extended to the edge of his left eye.

Devadatta pulled his hair back across his face and spoke to the Englishman. 'I know what you're thinking, my friend. How did a fine- looking character like me end up with two different faces? If only I had a thousand *rupees* for each time I've been asked.'

Saul listened as Devadatta explained the circumstances about how it had happened. He paused, as if turning pages of a familiar book in his mind, before un-folding the details. Surprisingly, Devadatta began by making a declaration; a statement about the good that had come from the incident. He had shaken off his arrogance and vanity; and in so doing, discovered more about his true self. All this, after an unfortunate encounter with the father of a local woman. With his usual self-assurance and charm, he had crawled into the affections of a young girl from a neighbouring village. She was blinded to his advances; seduced by the attraction of his empty promises.

Devadatta outlined his harrowing encounter. The girl's father had found them alone in one of his storage barns. Their compromising position enraged the father so much, that he reached for a pot of boiling oil, on the stove, nearby, and threw its content at Devadatta's face. At this point the victim of the tale smiled, as wryly as his disfigured face would permit. 'At least I managed to turn my head sufficiently to protect one side of my face.'.

As they discussed why this had happened, a tale unfolded of a vain and narcissistic man, with little respect for women. He had used his looks and charm to ingratiate himself into the lives of numerous females. He was oblivious to his own capricious selfishness. Saul could recognise another man in these actions. Himself. The location and cultures may have been different, but the issues were the same.

What was most interesting was Devadatta's response to all this. His seductive lifestyle and subsequent facial disfigurement had led to something of a transformation in his attitude to woman. Now that attractive females no longer looked at him in the same way, he had finally realised the importance of respect

112

for all women. The incident had been the catalyst for profound change. And ironically, his changed personality had led to the very thing that had escaped the grasp of his former self. Love. His new partner was more interested in who he was, rather than his physical appearance. He had become a better person, more in tune with what was of true importance in life.

Mohammed, meanwhile, was busy talking to a smart, well -dressed man, of athletic build. He initially seemed to be unaware of Mo's presence and was talking to the woman on his left. Mohammed sat there quietly, until, accidently dropping his fork, he felt the need to apologise for leaning across the stranger's plate.

'Excuse me,' he interjected, politely.

The man turned around and looked inquisitively at Mohammed. 'Oh Hello, I'm Prahlad' he announced. 'You must be the Muslim gentleman?' For a fleeting moment Mohammed panicked, as if his identity had been stolen, and pinned up on a noticeboard, for public display. But he also felt that quickening of the heart that first seized him in the canteen at work. When he met someone, who understood his secret.

Prahlad smiled, as if anticipating his reaction and explained that he had been invited to the meal to meet a Muslim man, from the UK. He himself, originated from a small town, further down the valley. Alan had suggested that the Londoner might find the events of Prahlad's recent life, interesting. He recounted the sad story of his banishment from home, after it emerged that Prahlad was gay. 'Although we have some of the most liberal laws about homosexuality anywhere in the world,' he exclaimed, 'This is rural Nepal. Intolerance and discrimination is still widespread here, just like in India. This is certainly not Kathmandu, my friend!'

As Mohammed listened, he found himself drawn into a familiar tale of deception, hostility and isolation. It transpired that when his homosexuality became known, Prahlad was forced out of the village; ostracised, cold-shouldered by his former friends and family.

'I was treated like some sort of social pollutant…' he continued, '…contaminating those around me and endangering the stability of family life. My *camouflage* marriage, they said, had brought shame and humiliation on my wife and her relatives. They gave me little choice, but to leave. The man I was having a relationship was less fortunate. A group of local vigilantes almost beat him to death. He had to be transferred to a hospital in Pokhara.' He looked at Mohammed and said 'I think you may understand me, more than most. Islam is every bit as unforgiving about such matters.'

Alan and Amit had started to gather the British visitors together, to leave.

Mohammed looked at Prahlad. A kindred spirit, in need of empathy? 'Thank you for sharing your experience with me. I think you realise that I face something similar in my own life, back home. I wish you every blessing and hope *Inshallah* that you find some peace in your heart'

Mohammed walked across to his British companions, reflecting on the human cost of acknowledging one's sexual identity. He also knew there were things to be done when he returned to Britain.

They arrived back at their lodgings as the sky started to turn the colour of blood, framed by banks of black, menacing cloud.

'Mm. Not a good sign,' Amit muttered to Alan.

24

Stormy skies

As they slept in their beds that night, the snow returned with a vengeance. It was unlike the modest falls that had decorated the landscape with Christmas charm, barely two days before. This time, giant snow-flakes filled the skies, delivered within the jaws of a ferocious storm. Powerful winds snapped at their refuge, seeking out any weak points in the precarious wooden structure. As they sheltered under its beams, fingers and toes began of ache with the numbness of the nocturnal cold.

Luke and Mohammed had been woken by the sound of a banging shutter, prised open, no doubt, by the howling gale. They found Alan downstairs, wrapped in a thick quilt. He had already dealt with the noisy wooden pane. Now, he sat at the window, peering anxiously at the spectacle, outside.

'Everything OK, Alan? It's freezing down here!', the Londoners exclaimed.

'Yes, Of course, my friends! Mother nature is giving us a real battering tonight! I'm sure it will blow over by the morning'

'Just listen to the wind! We've both found it difficult to sleep', Mohammed added. The lads fetched some warm water to drink from the kitchen stove. On their return they urged Alan to try to get some sleep himself and retreated to the warmth of their own beds.

Daylight broke and still the storm raged. It was difficult to see much beyond the outer fencing of the farm. Already, the wind had swept several drifts of snow up against the farm buildings. It was deeper than Mohammed had ever seen. As high as his waist, Luke shared. Still, Amit and Dexa summoned them to the breakfast table for some lumpy porridge and the much more appetising Tibetan bread. Luke had taken quite a fancy to this local delicacy. As they ate and re-fuelled their empty stomachs, Dexa and Alan spoke about their plans for the day.

'Clearly, we can't venture out today until the storm passes. It's taking longer than we thought so Dexa and I have a suggestion to make. We were going to do this tomorrow, but in the circumstances, perhaps we could bring it forward.

We wanted to introduce you to an important part of the cultural heritage of this region. Something that began life in the ancient monasteries of Buddhism. For thousands of years, the monks have developed a style of art that presents the doctrines of Buddhist culture for people through the medium of painted scrolls. We call it *Thangka* painting. These pictures carry the stories of how people understand the challenges of life. Dexa, here, has been studying these manuscripts and pictures for many years. She would like you all to join her in the construction of some new *Thangka's*. Pictures that are created to resonate with your own lives. When the weather clears, we will visit the Tibetan refugee village close by, to meet some of her friends. There, we will bless the *Thangka's*, in the traditional way. I think it will be very interesting for you to go there. This is the place where I first met Dexa. Some of her friends are trained *Thangka* monks who, like her, escaped from Chinese persecution. Meanwhile, let's see what Dexa has in store for us!'

They assembled in the dining room. Large pieces of blank canvas were piled up, next to wooden frames. Alongside them, clusters of brushes and several pots of paint and herbs, had been placed, nearby. Dexa reached down and lifted a large picture on to the table. 'This, she said, is my favourite *Thangka*. It reminds me of the challenges I face in my own life.' She pointed to the multi-faced central figure. This is *Avalokitesshvara*. He is an important *Bodhisattvas*; a spiritual being, representing compassion and pity. His many hands reach out to the world. He notices all the suffering out there and points towards how to alleviate the pain. When I reflect on my life, I find the words of the *mantra*: 'Om Mani Padre Hum', deeply significant.

'A *mantra* is a hypnotic chant that can assist us, strengthen our powers of concentration. Reciting these sounds, frees my mind to understand it's true purpose. These are so much more than just important words. *Om* is the basic sound of the universe, a vibration connecting the physical, spiritual and unconscious dimensions. *Mani* is a precious stone; a symbol for humanity. The *Padmi* is the lotus flower, rising from the muddy waters. It's a metaphor for our cleansing of the soul. Finally, the *Hum* represents the sacrifice of the self. Letting go of the things which damage us, so we can embrace endless compassion.'

Dexa paused, as if in prayerful contemplation.

Saul chose the moment to whisper in Luke's ear. 'I think I'm out of my depth here. Hope you're taking it all in!'

Luke tried to ignore him. He was engrossed. The others sat transfixed, in silence, attempting to absorb the meaning of her words.

Dexa looked at her foreign visitors, benignly and continued. 'To help us create a meaningful picture for ourselves, it is important to prepare properly. Focus the mind; meditate on how your individual life journey is unfolding. Try to see it as a sacred experience. But when we finish, we do not write our names on these pieces of work. The story may be ours, but the events depicted are not unique. They belong to all human beings. The person who reflects on the *Thangka* is only interested in the depiction itself because it's purpose is to teach and inspire others. I would like you to look at these examples I have brought along. Then, using some of the symbols in the pictures and some of your own ideas, try to create your own *Thangka*. One that reverberates with your own experience of life.

'I advise you to begin with background colours; light, sky and clouds. Then, add the main figures in darker colours. Please do not fill in the features of the faces. These are always completed later when the *Thangka* is consecrated at a special ceremony.

'Some final thoughts: what I am presenting to you is an individual instruction, which requires great attentiveness. Try to do this in silence to allow your thinking to focus on the task. Free your memories to explore the rich tapestry that life has woven for you. Celebrate the good things as well as the challenges. In a couple of hours, we will sound the gong to bring the activity to an end. I will be available in the corner of the room, if you require any help. In the meantime, I'll leave you to your *Thangka*'

With a respectful bow, she walked away from the table and sat next to the window.

25

Secrets in canvas and stone

The British visitors got out of their seats and made their way towards the materials, stacked in neat piles, at the end of the table. Chalk, paint, ornate bowls of minerals, mixed with animal glue, lime and plain cotton cloth. Alan remained with them, giving them the impression that he would also be taking part. They sifted through the numerous *Thangka's* that had been left as templates to help them. Another sheet of canvas was attached to the back of each, explaining the meaning of each figure in the painting.

Luke gazed at the figures in front of him. Closing his eyes, he imagined himself in the picture. When he opened them again, he reached for a dark piece of chalk and began to sketch. Some of the symbols he used were borrowed from the examples he looked at, but others were designed to represent the unhappy moments of his existence. As he applied the chalk and added pencil and paint, he felt his confidence starting to grow. His fingers formed an image of a seated *Buddha;* the hands positioned in a classic *mudra* or gesture of fearlessness, *abhaya.* This would be his theme.

The picture started to develop. He was climbing rocky clefts to reach his estranged daughter. An extended a hand of reconciliation towards his former wife and her partner, appeared alongside. He painted another figure, himself, travelling eight paths, towards a palace. Luke was reminded of the Buddhist teaching about suffering: follow the paths of righteousness. Each of his paths bore the name of one of these Buddhist values, articulated in the *Eight-fold path.* Three of them stood out in his *Thangka;* they were drawn as much wider routes. *Right intention, Right effort, Right mindfulness.* As they got closer to the palace, these three paths converged to form one route. It led up to the palace gate.

Luke put down his chalk stick and held up his picture. Twenty minutes later, his *Thangka* was adorned with a kaleidoscope of colours, highlighting his message. He knew what his drawing meant. He felt a renewed energy to embark upon what he now needed to do.

He looked around to see how the others were faring. Mohammed and Saul were sitting back in their chairs, appearing to have finished. Sarah was putting her brushes away and Gurdeep was still at work with a chalk stick. Alan was stretching his own completed *Thangka* across a wooden frame. They were interrupted by the piercing sound of the gong. As it reverberated around the dining room, everyone took the cue to wander off to freshen up. He couldn't speak for the others, but all this creative contemplation had given Luke quite an appetite.

After dinner, Dexa asked them how they had found the experience. Luke and Muhammed were keen to show the others their *Thangka* paintings. Although there was little artistic merit in their drawings, the ideas which emerged were important. Saul surprised some with his reflection on 'temptations of the flesh', while Gurdeep and Sarah presented more complex, spiritual stories.

Finally, Alan held up his *Thangka*. A beautiful metamorphosis of the human condition; ever changing, ever striving for perfection and enlightenment. Everybody found something in it to identify with. As they finished off their drinks, Alan asked them to take something away with them. A memento. It wasn't food! Dexa passed around a black polished stone to each member of the group. As each person took their stone she recited the *mantra* they had heard earlier. *'Om Mani Padre Hum'*

'Do you remember what I said earlier?' she said. 'About the *mani* stone? Let these precious rocks be your constant reminder of how precious your life is, and that of all humanity. If you find it helpful, write something upon it. One, or two words, which epitomise your challenges with this world. A constant reminder of your own suffering and your struggles to overcome it'

Each of them wandered up and took a stone. Some of them said they would think a little more about what to write and engrave the object later.

Luke was already busy with the gold paint and a small brush. He wrote the word 'courage' in large letters.

26

The village of memories

Luke awoke the next morning, to the bustling sounds of activity below him. There were several people milling around noisily, laying plates and cutlery in the dining room. From outside the building came other sounds; snow being scooped up by large wooden shovels and moved into piles. He scraped the frozen pane of his bedroom window with a piece of plastic card and looked out upon a new day. Amit was busy organising the clear up. The snow-storm was finally over.

Amit and Alan were in a positive mood, at breakfast. 'Look,' said Alan. 'The skies are clear. Today we go to the refugee village. We have sent messages to my friends there. They will be expecting us.'

Luke asked how long the journey would take.

'Normally, around half an hour,' replied Alan, 'but with all this snow, who knows!'

The British women did not look impressed. They could have easily spent another day in the warmth, developing their tangka painting skills.

An hour later, the small band of British travellers, accompanied by Alan, Amit and Dexa, were moving out of the farmstead, heading towards the southern ridge. At least, that was the plan! The wind had swept up giant snowdrifts during the night, to block their paths. They offered a series of formidable barriers to any living thing that wanted to cross this landscape. Trees, rocks, yes, even themselves, would sink beneath their camouflaged white disguises, if foolish enough to sit around, outside, for too long!

The speckled patterns of their foot-prints, left on the pristine ground, was the only evidence that they had been there. Luke noted two further sets of faded boot marks in front, leading off into the distance. Evidence that Alan's messengers had passed through recently.

Their own progress, however, was painfully slow. Only Amit and Dexa had any real experience of navigating their way through such drifts before and, although it had stopped snowing, it remained bitterly cold. For Luke and his former flatmates, it was simply exhausting. The wide-rimmed plastic 'hammer' caps, fixed to the tip of their trekking poles, at least helped to prevent them falling over. Luke became aware that Sarah, Gurdeep and Mohammed were starting to lag. Their efforts were beginning to take their toll.

Amit, as always, missed little of what was happening around him. He needed to stop regularly, so he could clear a path through the deeper sections. But it also provided a good opportunity for the rest of them to catch their breath. 'Let's rest, here for a few minutes,' he implored them. Their silence confirmed the decision. They had already been gone from the house for nearly an hour and seemed no closer to their destination. Sensing their anxiety, Alan shouted across to the group that it would not take too much longer.

Luke looked at the high peaks that flanked their corridor through the snow. His daughter might imagine them as enormous portions of ice-cream that had been pushed into biscuit cones; somehow not quite fitting their toppings. He welcomed the distraction. Much of the snow was hanging, precariously, in sheets, over the high edges. He could hear Ellen saying to him 'It would take an army of children to lick these away, Dad!' He chuckled to himself at the frivolous thought.

They hoisted their day-packs back onto their frames and continued to move on, trying to ignore the cold wind that swirled around them. It wasn't wise to linger for too long. It seemed to Luke that the wind was on a singular mission; to grasp every exposed part of their bodies and pummel them, to weaken their resolve. But this was no survival game. Not yet! Just, when most of them were struggling to feel any evidence of blood circulating around their toes, a ghostly outline of buildings appeared on the horizon. Behind them, the protective walls of Annapurna Two, stood imposing and proud.

Luke stared at the village in front of him. Each building was a replica of the one next to it. The roofs seem to be held together by rolls of frost- covered string; connected, intricately, like some enormous spiders' web. Jagged-toothed icicles had formed giant stalactites to decorate the outer beams. They sparkled in the midday sun.

'Menlung', Alan shouted. 'The village of memories.'

As they trundled into the frozen streets of this community of forgotten souls, suspicious eyes tracked their every movement, from behind thick curtains. They didn't get many visitors from Europe, Alan had informed them earlier. As they drew nearer, a closer inspection revealed that these houses were much more functional in design, than they had seen in other parts of Nepal. More like log cabins, as if constructed with the sole purpose of simply providing basic shelter. No more than that. A place, Luke thought, where you wouldn't want to linger any longer than you had to.

They learned later, that it was built as a temporary settlement for displaced refugees to rest and eventually move on from. That was in 1974. But very few had moved on. It had become a permanent home for most of them. There was nowhere else for its inhabitants to go.

'Some call this the *village of skeletons*, where it's inhabitants leave only their bones,' said Amit. 'But we prefer to call it the *village of memories*; a place where our brothers and sisters from the other side of the *Himalaya* can remember who they once were, in peace and freedom. Come, we are heading to the house over there'. He pointed to a large building, adorned with faded prayer flags, in front of them. Two elderly women stood outside the door, without coats; oblivious, it seemed, to the bone chilling weather. Dexa greeted them enthusiastically and embraced them like long lost relatives. 'This is Jampa and Lobsang,' she announced. 'My Tibetan friends; and now, part of my family, in Nepal. They do not speak English, but I'll interpret. You can ask them any questions you may have. I am happy to translate for you.'

She broke into local Nepalese dialect and explained to the women that these visitors, pointing to the shivering group, were Alan's friends from England. They bowed their heads greeted their visitors with a formal gesture.

Ten minutes later, they were all sat around the wooden fire, clasping hot cups of tea, as much for the warmth, as to quench their thirst. Sarah attracted Dexa's attention, with a question. 'How long they have been living here?' she asked.

Dexa turned to the older of the two women to check. Jampa's austere features looked as if they had been chiselled directly from the harsh, mountain rock. After a brief exchange, Dexa turned to Sarah and said: 'Jampa has been here since 1996 and her friend, Lobsang, came here fifteen years ago. Both looked as if they were now well into their seventies.

Gurdeep remarked to Sarah that the two elderly women could be taken for sisters.

Lobsang pulled her silver hair back behind skeletal shoulders and whispered into Dexa's ear. Dexa listened carefully, nodding, in support.

After a few minutes, Dexa had finished translating what Lobsang had said. The local woman was keen to share it with the rest of them. Dexa translated her words. 'We entered this country as refugees, many years ago and will always be grateful to the people of Nepal for their kindness and support. The government of this land built this place for us and we have tried to make a life here. Things have not been easy. Although we receive a small sum of money each month from the government, it barely keeps us from starvation. Even so, we consider ourselves fortunate. Not a day goes by without us thinking about our former lives in Tibet and we people we were parted from. Life under Chinese rule provided most of us with little option but to make the treacherous journey over the mountains. Like Dexa, we were forced to leave loved ones behind. Yes, there were tears, but at least we now enjoy some freedom. However, we are a displaced people and don't really see ourselves as Nepalese. In this country, there are more than two million souls who cannot claim citizenship. We are among them. The rules are strict. Unless we learn to write and speak Nepalese; engage in recognised employment and renounce our Tibetan citizenship, we cannot be recognised as sons and daughters of this country. We cannot vote. We have few legal rights'.

Luke thought it was a moving testimony and wondered how he'd cope if he were never to see Debbie and Ellen again. As if sensing the growing sombre atmosphere, Dexa led the party through the front of the house to a back room. 'Come, let us eat. You must be hungry.'

Saul and Mohammed were surprised to see meat on the menu. Almost everything they had eaten so far was vegetarian. But here, was a dark meat, competing with the usual vegetables, spices and delicacies, for a prominent place on the table. After such a tiring trek, the attraction of hot meat was, thought Mohammed, more than appealing. It smelt delicious.

'Amit', enquired Saul. 'What is this meat. I don't recognise it?

'This, my friend, is Yak!

'But I thought the Nepalese, Buddhist or Hindu, were vegetarians?

'Indeed, we are, but the providence of nature sometimes throws up dilemmas to those of us who do not eat meat. Yesterday, was such a day.'

Saul looked perplexed.

'What I mean, is that if the Gods decree that the body of one of his creatures should suddenly perish, it becomes expedient for us to utilise the carcass. We help to liberate its *atman* or soul. After all, it's spirit has now moved on to another life form. Like us when we perish, the body no longer has a purpose. This is the mystery of reincarnation. As for this yak, it plunged off a mountain pass to its death, yesterday. We eat it's flesh in celebration of its life. Nothing will go to waste. Already the hair, skin and bones are being fashioned into garments and household equipment. It is what the beast would want,' he said confidently. It is also what the gods would want'

None of the English contingent felt like challenging what they had heard. In such a desolate place, it seemed a powerful argument. The fact that nothing had tasted so good to them for such as long, was more a statement about how hungry they were, rather than a preference for meat. Only Gurdeep resisted the temptation to indulge. Her vegetarian principles didn't extend to Buddhist pragmatism.

Meanwhile, Dexa, Alan, and Amit had fallen into conversation with the two elderly female villagers. Another man, looking bedraggled from his own journey, that day, was wearing a thick animal-skinned coat, with matching gloves and hat. He had joined them from the back door. He looked keen to cast aside the chills of his journey as he warmed himself at the fire. Luke was intrigued by his body language. He was gesticulating wildly, with his stick. Something was clearly troubling him. After a while, Alan gathered his visitors around and spoke to them.

'Our hosts are a little concerned about our journey back. That man over there has just returned from the path we followed to get here. He was rounding up some stray goats, when he heard a loud, cracking sound above him. To his left, a section of overhanging snow had broken away from the top and started to hurtle down the walls of the mountain. Luckily for him, its direction took the snow away from where he and his goats were, but shot across the valley floor, right through the mountain track. Although only a small avalanche, it had blocked the route into the village, about a kilometre away. The path would need digging out before it could be used again'.

It must have been his new-found strength speaking, fortified by all that yak protein, but Saul expressed the desire to grab a shovel and get out there, straight away. Alan, however, was in far more cautious mode. 'We need to be careful, Saul. This fall might not be the only avalanche in the vicinity. From what the herdsman said, it's going to require more than a few spades to clear this blockage. We're going to need the considerable strength of a couple of large yaks to bulldoze their way through. That is why Jampa and Lobsang have suggested you all stay in the village tonight. We can make a start on this, first thing in the morning.'

Sarah's eyes scanned their modest dwelling, making a mental note of the absence of beds, before exclaiming 'Where, exactly, do you mean, Alan?'

Jampa whispered something to Dexa. She explained what was obvious to the party. They wouldn't all be able to stay there, with her, but Lobsang and another of her friends, Norbu, would each accommodate a couple of them in their homes.

Saul caught sight of the afternoon sky, through a gap in the curtains. Clouds had already mushroomed across the blue firmament, obscuring the menace of the high places above. 'Which of you lucky ladies, gets to share with me, tonight, then? he bellowed, confidently, across to Sarah and Gurdeep.

'I think I'd prefer to share with one of the yaks, Saul. No offence!'

Sarah's repost brought some much, needed laughter to the situation. Behind their grins and cheery bravado, the uncertainty of fear had slowly begun to creep in. None more so than with Amit, who had gone noticeably quiet during the discussions. His mind was still pre-occupied with the avalanche that had blocked their route home.

PART THREE

Tears in the Snow

27

Trapped

They retreated to their separate huts that night, while an uneasy stillness descended upon the valley. Although they were effectively trapped by the snow, there were some encouraging signs. The wind outside, had dropped and the old, rusting thermostat, that had been hammered into a post outside Jampa's porch, was indicating a slight rise in temperature. Their hosts had arranged for Saul and Mohammed to lodge with Lobsang. Gurdeep and Sarah would be staying with Jampa. Dexa and Amit, meanwhile, knowing several people in *Menlung*, had disappeared to make their own preparations to bed down for the night.

Alan and Luke went to a building just around the corner, owned by a man called Tamzin. Luke was a little surprised when their Tibetan host for the night, addressed them in almost perfect English. 'I learned your language, while working as a trekking guide', he told him, as they made up extra beds in his house. 'From a group of very fine English speakers - they were all German!' He broke into a broad smile and his humour was not lost on his English visitor.

Luke retorted with his own banter. His host, he said, carried the only Himalayan name he knew before coming out on the trip. 'You know', Luke continued, confidently, 'Tamzin, like the Indian guide who was with Edmund Hilary in 1953, at Everest. I thought you would be older!'

Tamzin looked puzzled. It was clear he hadn't been following Luke's train of thought on this one. 'Oh, that Tamzin', the owner eventually replied, with a raised eyebrow. I think you're confusing my name with that of a famous Sherpa called Tenzing Norgay. I am named after somebody even more important than him and he isn't even Indian! Born, here in Nepal. Yes. I am named after none other than the *Dalai Lama*. What you may not know, Mr Luke, is that Tamzin is the first name of the *Dalai Lama* and as such, the most popular modern name in Tibet! Pretty popular here, too! Both boys and girls are proud to carry his name!'

'As are those who are named Tenzing,' he added as an afterthought.

Luke grimaced with the exposure of his ignorance and made a mental note to do a bit more background reading next time, to avoid putting his foot in it, again! He had already decided earlier, to make a mental note of some of Tamzin's little jewels of information, before scuttling off to the back of the room, looking for his rucksack to find his i-pad, or failing that, a pen and notepad.

When Luke reappeared, Alan was standing near the front door, in his boots and coat, ready to leave. Tamzin was recounting their conversation, telling him he'd been elevated to the status of world -famous mountain guide! Alan smiled, pulled up his hood and said he needed to talk to one of the villagers, but would be back later. Before he left, he turned to Luke and said, 'Did I mention, Luke, that Tamzin's son is studying the history of high altitude climbing, as part of his degree course, in Kathmandu?' it seemed the young man's father had read every book on the course, he had brought home because his own knowledge had been limited to guiding Europeans through less dramatic climbs than *Sagarmatha or* Mount Everest, as they knew it. Once upon a time he would have given everything for the opportunity that came Tenzing's way, to make history with Edmund Hillary. But that was in the past.

The two remaining men closed the door behind Alan and sat down by the fire. Luke watched the embers dancing around the rim of the glowing hearth. He looked across at Tamzin, who looked to be in reflective mood. 'You know, Luke, Tenzing Norgay wasn't that different from us, especially during his early life. Like you and I, he journeyed here from another country. His parents, like me, came from Tibet. They settled as yak herders, near the Khumbu valley. He wanted to know more about the meaning of life and at one stage, began training as a Buddhist monk at Tengboche monastery. He too was a searcher. His name meant 'carrier of the Buddhist Dharma'. But his destiny lay elsewhere, and he left the monastery and travelled to Darjelling, in India. Eventually, he found his destiny among the highest mountains on earth. Maybe, your friend Alan, in his own way, has travelled a similar road too', he ventured.

Luke sipped the mug of ginger tea and listened to this comparison. He found himself absorbed by the words of his wise and knowledgeable host. He also realised that slowly but surely, he too, was being drawn into the magic of this mountain kingdom.

28

A mountain awakes

It must have been about one in the morning, when it happened. Luke had a recollection of suddenly waking up with a jolt. He was sweating. Later, he tried to extract a clearer memory of what occurred, but could only vaguely recall a pulsating, crashing sound in his head; a noise which grew progressively louder with each second that passed. At least, he thought that was what he had experienced, for he was barely awake.

Then, darkness. And nothing. That was as much as he could remember. A river of rock, ice and snow, had come crashing down upon them, colliding with and over-whelming the village buildings. It was almost instantaneous. His flimsy bed was pummelled with innumerable lumps of ice and rocks. The slumbering dreams of another day's adventure had been brought to a terrifying halt. They had been savaged by the sudden appearance of an unexpected nightmare. A monster had been summoned from the mountain tops and its gifts were death and destruction. His room, littered with a tsunami of unwanted debris, was now unrecognisable.

From the heart of the mountain that lay behind the *village of memories,* a white sea had poured down over the village. Disgorged in a few terrifying moments, with barely an opportunity to jump from their beds. There was no escape. Their survival hung on a thread of fate. No-one anticipated the avalanche coming. 'Well you wouldn't, would you, at that time of the morning?' Luke reflected, afterwards.

It had torn a path through the high valleys and plummeted down upon them with the speed of a high-performance engine. Some say you can hear an avalanche coming. Not one like this.

Something solid must have collided with Luke. Something so hard that all he could remember about what happened was wiped away in an instant. Everything turned black. There was only white dust and wreckage to witness what followed.

As if lifted from the bowels of the earth, a new day was being dragged through the dawn. Dark, morning clouds were hovering, ominously, outside, but Luke, nor any of the others could see them. The vapours of destruction had obscuring the morning light, choking the sun's rays into a premature exit. What was happening beneath, under the sky, would have been difficult for anybody to watch. Even the birds were silent, as if humbled into stillness by the loss of so many vanished trees. Once familiar farm-land sounds had disappeared from the air, leaving only the faint echo of rock and earth, still re-settling, re-moulding, into new shapes and forms.

Luke eventually woke from the safety of his unconsciousness. He tried to ignore the intermittent sounds of crunching and cracking, reverberating around his eardrums. It felt like the ground was still moving. Whatever had survived the impact of the avalanche was still on the move, gauging out the new contours of an alien, landscape. Fortunately for Luke, he was still alive in it. The smell of fresh soil and shattered stone, invaded his nostrils, making him feel nauseous. At least it kept a far more toxic smell at bay. The unpalatable stench of death.

He wiped the flaky dust from his eyes and tried to stand up. A sharp pain shot down his left leg and he reached out an arm to steady himself. A mistake. The imbalance sent him tumbling back to the debris that lay, strewn across the floor. As he fell, Luke caught his elbow on a protruding metal rod, before hitting the ground with a thud. A gaping cut emerged, accompanied by all the sudden pain such wounds can muster. He reached for his pocket and found a tissue to stem the blood. Worryingly, this was not the only example of crimson gore he could identify on his body. The source of the discomfort in his leg could now be viewed clearly: a badly lacerated ankle, bleeding below the torn hem of his jeans. Luke gritted his teeth and tried not to panic. This, he thought, was easier said than done, as the throbbing pain from his elbow now competed with sporadic spasms of mounting discomfort from the damaged leg.

'Hello', he cried out nervously. 'Can anybody hear me?'

The muffled sounds of another life form murmured in the corner of the room. His first thought was: Is it Alan? In the dark and dust, it was impossible to identify its source, but it seemed to emanate from somewhere on his left. Again, he repeated the question and this time, Luke pin-pointed its location.

'Here. Over here!', came a faint response. Among the creaking of misplaced roof-beams and lumps of plaster, he identified the sound of a man's voice. 'Please! Help Me! I can't move!'

Eventually, Luke pulled himself up again and dragged his damaged limb across to the corner of the room. Each obstacle he was forced to pull himself over, brought the fresh throbbing of new pain. It had sounded like the voice of a man, he thought. He looked more closely at the ghostly figure on the floor. The beard confirmed its gender. He didn't immediately identify him, but it definitely wasn't

Alan. Too short. Too much hair. Whoever it was, he was covered in plaster and dust. More worryingly, a large wooden beam had fallen from the roof and lodged itself across the man's torso. Although he couldn't see signs of specific injury, the man seemed to be held fast, crushed beneath the weight of the wood. With difficulty, he grabbed hold of the beam and with a colossal push, tried to manoeuvre the wooden support away. Despite herculean efforts, the perilously dangling beam, failed to release its grip on the man. At least it moved sufficiently to view the prostrate figure more clearly.

'Mr Luke, it's Tamzin. Please. Help me. I beg you!'

Luke slumped back to the floor and tried to think what to do next. As Luke sat there on the ground, he began to hear sounds of anxious voices outside. He called out and listened, as a combination of shovels and bare hands burrowed towards him. It seemed an age, but the eventual sight of those excited faces when they broke through, would remain with him, always. Like angels calling him back from the dead.

An age later Luke sat on a piece of broken log, sipping hot tea. A young, women stood next to him. She herself bore the evidence of injury; with a bandage around the head. She was cleaning his wounds. No doubt, another victim among many, in this make-shift 'triage' of damaged bodies. He had been luckier than many. Apart from his puncture injury to his shoulder and a damaged ankle, he was ok. Sore, but alive! Looking around what remained of the village, he could locate barely half a dozen buildings still standing. Most of the others were at least partially buried under snow and ice. Some had completely vanished, leaving only a carpet of snow and broken wood to testify to what existed barely twelve hours before. Over to his left, in what he guessed remained of Lobsang's home, there was only an eerie silence.

Across from their tent, the joyous cries of his rescuers had given way to the desperation of the bereaved. Small groups of people, huddled together, in despondency, to shed their tears. He identified one of them as Sarah. As if sensing his gaze and connected by telegraphic grief, she turned towards him and cried out. With the aid of a stray branch, he hobbled across to greet her. 'Oh, Luke', she cried, with a hug; pregnant with the anticipation of sharing her shocking news. 'You're alive! Thank God!

She turned away from him, as if incapable of adding to what she wanted to say. She knew the words that followed would devastate her former flatmate. 'I'm afraid Saul…He didn't make it'.

Luke looked at her in dis-belief. Unable to process the revelation that his best friend; his only real friend in this world, was dead. He looked down at the row of lifeless bodies on the ground. Instead of the confident face of his North London pal, there was a pale replica of the person he knew and loved. He started to well-up himself, as the visual impact of his loss, registered. With tears streaming down his cheeks, he gazed at the two deep gashes that had scourged Saul's face. In addition, his torso, seemed to have born, the brunt, of some terrible crush. Shocking as the sight was, all he could think about was how Saul would have reacted if he was still able to stand alongside him. He would have joked about the possible disfigurement of his face and how his new friend from the restaurant would have called the two of them 'twins. Peas from the same pod.'

Saul would have used his considerable energy to push them away from his corpse. 'Stop gawking and go and do something useful, like helping to dig out more casualties, rather than standing here, crying' Maybe Saul had his weaknesses. There would certainly be some women back at home who wouldn't mourn his demise. But here, in this place of devastation, Luke desperately wanted to indulge in, to clutch on to something positive. That optimism and thirst for life, which he knew Saul once offered to the world. It was strange how so many examples of this now flooded back into his head. The times he had organised his social life for him, after leaving university; his encouragement during the initial pursuit of Debbie; his support when Luke crumbled, when faced with the loss of his wife. In many ways, Saul was the big brother he had always wanted. He was going to miss him more than his old friend could possibly know.

Shaken back to reality, Luke inquired about the others. Sarah shared the details known to her. Mohammed had been badly injured, almost buried in Lobsang's hut. He had suffered a complex fracture in his right leg and his left arm was so badly broken that it might have to be amputated. Gurdeep had a head -wound but was going to be okay. She was being treated over in the large tent. As for Alan, nothing had been seen or heard.

There was some positive news, though. A couple of the Tibetan women had told them that Alan had *gone,* presumably, to get help. Luke was troubled with this. His rescuers had searched the remains of Tamzin's house for survivors and pulled the owner from the beam that had trapped him. They had also checked the remains of the other properties. Alan was no-where to be seen. Nor Amit.

Another familiar face appeared on the stretcher, being carried past them. Despite her crushed body, Luke and Gurdeep instantly recognised her by her silver locks. It was Dexa. Sadly, 'she who teaches' would never deliver another lesson or offer words of wisdom to someone in need. Her time had come. She had died in her beloved *Himalaya* albeit, on the wrong side of *Everest*. Sarah was sure she was being mourned by some special people, far away in Tibet.

Amit eventually appeared, supported by several local farmers and shepherds. His heart was heavy. He looked like a man, ready to burst into pieces; each one soaked in his tears. 'My friends, what has this mountain done to us. What have we done to bring upon us so much sorrow and pain?'

Sarah checked if he was ok.

'Yes, Miss Sarah, I have survived with just a few bruises. But what is the situation here now? When I left the village earlier, to find more people to help with the digging, there were many people buried. These men with me, will help us look for anybody still missing. Luke knew there was one of their party still unaccounted for. He just had to approach Amit about him.

'Amit, Is Alan with you? Luke asked. 'Some of the villagers indicated he had *gone*. We assumed he was with you, seeking help'.

This information transformed Amit's face. He appeared to visibly shrink, as his features crumpled with the possibility of news he could barely contemplate.

'No', he replied. 'He wasn't with me. I thought he was here?'

The tension was not helped by the failure to locate the women who had earlier reported him *gone*.

Luke wracked his fragile head to try to remember if he had seen Alan return to Tamzin's hut the previous evening. He was sure he would have heard him arrive back. After all, he'd need to open that creaky old front door. One of them would have heard him. But he couldn't remember him returning. He realised that he even didn't know where, in the house, Alan was supposed to be sleeping. There were two main rooms and several alcoves: how could he avoid seeing him? Luke's mind desperately re-constructed the lay-out for answers.

'Go back and check the ruined house', Amit shouted to them. 'Find those women. Take another look at the row of bodies lying in the centre of the village', he instructed them, urgently. Luke chose the latter task. Several bodies were facing the ground and their numbers had grown. But with the resulting identification of each head, he slowly clawed back a little more hope that his old flat-mate was still alive.

'Alan's not here. He must be ok. He probably had arrangements to make, early this morning. I was no doubt, still asleep when he left'.

There was one man, of course, who should be able to verify this. Tamzin. Luke crossed the village square to the make-shift medical centre, set up, in one of the few buildings to survive, intact. At the rear of the hall lay Tamzin, prostrate on an old mattress, with his left leg and chest area heavily bandaged. He didn't look good. Luke leaned over the man and quietly called out his name. The patient was barely awake but stared inquisitively at his visitor.

'Tamzin, Tamzin, can you hear me? Luke beseeched him. 'Alan. Do you know what happened to Alan? Did he return, late to your house, last night?

The man from Menlung looked up and tried to shake his head.

'I'm sorry. I don't know. I can't remember anything that happened'.

29

Beyond the Jagged Boulder

The morning faded away and afternoon sunshine started to melt some of the surface snow. The mood of the community remained sombre. Everybody had gathered in the centre of Menlung, carrying what little they had grabbed from the ruins of their homes.

Amit spoke to the villagers in their local tongue. He thanked them for their generous hospitality; for sharing what little had been salvaged from the damaged village. On behalf of the British visitors, there were offerings of condolence to the families who had lost loved ones. They had shared in the loss with the death of one of their own and the injuries sustained by other members of the group. He finished by asking if he could have a few words with the women who claimed they had seen Alan. Nobody else seemed to know what had happened to him.

Luke feared the worse when two local women, still visually drowning in the sorrow of their own bereavement, stepped forward to speak to Amit. They were pointing towards the edge of the village where a large boulder of black rock marked the perimeter of the settlement. There was something in their manner that made Amit extremely concerned. What did they mean when they said he was lost?

Sarah panicked and ran off in the direction they were pointing to. Luke did his best to follow her, hobbling, with his stick. They found Sarah weeping, as she stood over the snow-covered body of a man, lying behind the rock. He was roughly her own age. He looked so peaceful. The European features and wispy beard only confirmed what she had already feared. It was their missing friend. Their benefactor, for what should have been the trip of their lives. Someone who had been their inspiration, during that last week. Alan Rogers. A man, un-recognisable from the immature flat-mate who drifted in and out of their life, a decade ago. The women were right: he had gone. Caught up in the chaos of this mountain nightmare. Trapped, or maybe thrown behind this strange, twisted outcrop of rock. Luke stared at the figure lying in the snow. Was Alan trying to seek the protection of the rock; attempting to outrun the fury of a terrifying wall of ice and snow? A pointless gesture, surely? There could have been no chance to escape its deadly clutches.

Amit appeared at the edge of the scene and sank to his knees. His tears framed a picture of heartache and despair. He was still there, twenty minutes later, like a guardian angel, mourning the loss of his English friend. 'What was he doing, lying so far from the house? What had happened to him? Did he meet with someone? Amit's questions were not directed to anyone, but himself. He needed to force them from his lips, to come to terms with the trauma of the moment.

He started to shout to the others who had gathered. 'Did he take a late-night walk and was caught in the avalanche? What happened to you, my friend?'

They would never find out. But all that mattered now, was that he was dead. Sarah and Luke fetched a white tunic and placed it over his poor, bruised body. A makeshift stretcher transported Alan to the centre; to take his place in the parade of the death, where the middle of the village once stood.

They knew was that they had lost a special person. A once, treasured flatmate who had dragged them out for a reunion at the far end of the world. An adventure that wasn't supposed to end like this.

Amit, however, had lost more than just an acquaintance. He knew had been parted from a soul friend; a spiritual companion, upon whose narrow shoulders, such dreams had been planned.

Sarah hadn't prayed for some time. But raising her eyes to the sky, she summoned words to bless his passing from this world: 'If there is such a thing as reincarnation', she petitioned, 'May his soul find rest in a new form, a body which will carry on his inspirational work. In this land of wisdom and awesome beauty, may you rest in peace, Alan.'

Meanwhile, there was a commotion back in the square, as several men, some with horses and carts, had appeared in the village. They looked anxious. Their frantic shouts needed little interpretation. They were looking for help. With a mixed diet of Nepalese, Tibetan and the occasional English word, they were asking for volunteers to go with them to the neighbouring village of Tansong. Many people had been buried by a mud-slide there, which had consumed most of the village. It hadn't even occurred to Luke that they were unlikely to be the only victims of this disaster. Later, he learned the full impact of what had happened across the valley, but for now, there was urgency in their pleas for help. There was now little left for him to do here.

Amit was already gathering support from those around him who had not been seriously injured. 'No Luke, you stay here', he implored him. Look after Mohammed, Gurdeep and Sarah.'

'Not me', Sarah responded defiantly. 'The least that lucky buggers like us can do, is to help these poor souls. Look around you! Many of them have given plenty of their own help here, this morning'

Luke spotted a pony and cart, at the edge of the village square. 'If I can hitch a lift in that,' he said to Sarah, 'I'll join you. I still have one good hand for digging!'

'Okay. If you want to', Amit responded.

Luke, rather gingerly, hoisted himself up, into the back of the cart, with some help from Sarah. Several local men squeezed in, alongside him. Tansong was only ten minutes down the snow-packed track.

If Menlung was an image of white-world destruction, then Tansong caste a brown shadow over the adjoining valley. Luke had never seen anything like it. From the edge of the village it looked like the hill behind had simply collapsed, shedding its deadly cocktail of saturated mud and rock to pour over the people of the village. They could make out the wailing of traumatised adults and children, desperate to find their loved ones. Entering the edge of where the village once stood, distraught people wandered aimlessly like they had emerged, formed from the womb, of this muddy abyss.

As Luke and Sarah disembarked, they stood for a moment, stupefied by the devastating sight before them. Still clasping the branch that he had used as a crutch in Menlung, Luke limped his way to what was left of the nearest buildings. He joined two of the men as they dug with their bare hands, through the brown slime. His effort, with only one limb was more symbolic than effective, but he had made his point. Sarah made her way to the medical centre that was packed with traumatised adults and damaged children.

The rescue attempts were already in progress. After some frantic digging around the dilapidated remains of one home, Luke and his companions heard buried voices. This drama was being played out at regular intervals, as survivors did all that was humanly possible to attract the attention of those who were looking for them. Whenever a tiny pocket of air was exposed, hopes would be temporarily raised. As the incarcerated victims started to be released from their frozen tombs, the rescuers sang their cries of exhilaration. These echoed, defiantly, across the late afternoon sky. The Englishman joined them in this gesture of defiance. A miracle against the odds. Human life plucked from the jaws of certain death. Just like he had been. Like the healing tones of medication, it calmed his traumatised mind and offered some form of redemption to the chaos of the day. It gave him a reason to carry on.

30

New Horizons

Luke stood, precariously on the edge of the temple steps. Keeping his balance with just the one arm, required concentration. The other limb was temporarily 'out of order', in a plaster-cast and held in a sling. At least he had regained the use of both legs again. He watched the monkeys leaping around, playfully, among brightly painted pillars. A momentary distraction. He wasn't here to watch them. He had other business in Patan. It had nothing to do with the Hindu temples and shrines. The sights of Kathmandu had lost their appeal. Below him, lay the Bagmati river, shimmering in the sunlight. From up here, it looked almost tranquil. But he knew what lay beneath its surface. Something Luke could barely grasp. The surrounding air was heavy with the aroma of flowers and incense. They competed for the challenge of trying to reduce the impact of another odour, wafting up, stealing a path towards him, from below. He remembered where he'd first experienced it. Menlung. It was the stench of death. Not those slightly unpleasant smell you sometimes get, when discovering a dead bird or mammal in the garden. This could not be swiftly deposited into a wheelie-bin. No. This was the un-mistakable smell of human decay; bodies ceremoniously laid out in their farewell gestures to the world.

He watched small clusters of people standing on the banks of the river, composing their final words of goodbye. Rehearsals, maybe, for these bystanders about to perform their rituals at life's ultimate drama. He would shortly join them. Their only comfort, lay in knowing that what the fires did not consume, the waters would carry away. There would be little left but ashes. On a journey, into re-incarnation, Dexa might have said. Luke could feel their loss; his loss. A sense of oblivion.

He had never been to a Hindu cremation before. Gurdeep and Sarah had decided not to attend. It was simply too much for them to watch Alan's body burnt in full view; his bones, to be discarded into the river. In truth, it was almost too much for Luke to endure. Amit clasped his 'good' arm and the two of them descended the steps to the cremation area. Amit turned to Luke and spoke, gently to the Englishman. 'I too, was surprised when he told me about this, Luke. I knew Alan had been deeply affected by Hindu and Buddhist culture, but to insist that when his time came, he would be ceremoniously laid out, like a Hindu, ready to embark upon the next stage of his existence, is remarkable. When he told me this, last year, I laughed about the idea of me outliving him. Look in the will, I've had drawn up', he told me. 'And remember the promise we made to each other about the lodge. Our place between the mountains. The idea must live on, even if, or when, I cannot be around to see it blossom. It was almost as if he knew something like this might happen, one day.'

It was now almost time for the cremation. Luke gazed down at the rows of neatly stacked blocks of wood, arranged on grey, stepped plinths, or *ghats*, beside the river. He started to count them. Possibly, twelve. Alongside, there were a dozen or so human carcasses, wrapped in white shrouds. lying next to ancient, stone steps. Alan, his friend, was one of them. It was true, he hadn't converted to any of these indigenous religions. He wasn't really a Hindu, a Buddhist or anything else for that matter, as far as they knew. Not officially, anyway. Just someone embracing death like his local friends would have done. An outsider adopting their customs, to emphasis, probably, his respect for them. Maybe they shouldn't have been so surprised at the arrangements. He had been more at home here than anywhere else in his life.

Alan had told Luke that this trip would change his life. He hadn't been wrong. But Luke didn't expect it to end like this. There should have been heart-felt farewells, embraces and promises to keep in touch. Instead only this. The salutations of the bereaved. Fixing his gaze on the dark pools of water, as they gently flowed away from the shore, he wondered how he had avoided being part of this flotilla of human decay. He watched the priest respectfully offering his final prayers, as the pyre was ignited. The flames quickly consumed the body of his friend. Within thirty minutes there was little left. Just bones and ash. He wondered again; *Why have I been spared?* As he bent down and scooped the ashes into a simple container. His make-shift urn would return to the UK. There were people who might want to remember. His parents, maybe. They would need to know how he came to end up on such a funeral pyre. In such a place as this.

Luke attended the inquest, in Pokhara. So, did Sarah and Gurdeep. The three of them had delayed their return to Britain for a few days. Only Mohammed made the flight. His injuries required further surgery. Once he had been given medical permission to fly home, he was flown back to London. There had been complications. They saved the leg but could not save his arm. Mohammed had cheated death by a whisker. He was just grateful to be alive. Luke found out later, when he visited him, that his family had rallied around. The drama of his fall from grace was temporarily forgotten. Even Fatima seemed to have forgiven him, he'd said. The last he heard, they were trying to make another go of it. Mo promised to keep in touch and let them know how it was all working out.

Luke sat between Sarah and Gurdeep, holding a hand from each one of them. The local administrator read out a long description of what had happened that fateful morning. How an earth tremor had triggered the avalanche and indirectly, destabilised the surrounding mountains. They called it a slab, avalanche. A large section of the ridge had fractured, with the weight of the snow breaking off and releasing a vast fall of snow and ice. They talked about the speed of such an event. How the debris can slide down the mountain-tops at speeds, reaching 130 kilometres per hour.

'Too much information,' thought Sarah. She didn't want a science lesson. The description would have been impressive, if it had simply been the findings of a technical investigation. But the wreckage of the phenomenon had torn so many loved ones from their friends and family. Three villages had been flattened. Two, directly due to the avalanche and one, because of a landslide that had followed. In total, fifty-eight people had died. Over a hundred had been injured, many seriously. Among them were three of their old flatmates and people like Dexa, who Luke and the others had come to cherish in those few days they had known her. Each of the victims were read out by name, against a background of gentle weeping in the public area.

Amit sat next to Sarah, gazing ahead, blindly. He was already thinking about the challenges that lay before him. Alan had spoken about it often enough. If anything was to happen to him, Amit must proceed with their plan. With the development of the mountain refuge. He was to move his family in to *Sanctuary*. Make it their home too. There was plenty of room. But did he have the heart for it, without Alan? At that precise moment, he doubted it. Yes: the deeds to the property had his name on them. The task now was his. He needed to make Alan's dream happen. There would be no Dexa, nor Alan, nor others, who were once connected with the place, to help him. They, like many, had perished. His head was spinning. Alan was depending upon him to carry on this work. Individuals, no matter how important they had been, would need to be replaced.

There was someone else who now had a deep connection with *Sanctuary*. He stood outside the government building, waiting for Amit to make his exit. The Annapurna farmer eventually appeared on the steps and saw Luke loitering. 'I've been thinking, Amit, he said. 'You are going to need some help with running *Sanctuary*. I was wondering if I might be of some use? Like Alan, I know I can't be here all the time. But I would love to return and provide some support to you. In honour of our friend. It would be my tribute to him'

Amit threw his arms around Luke and hugged him. 'Luke. That would raise my spirit in a way I can't describe. You will be welcome here any time. These events have forged a bond between us that will never be broken. Come back to us soon.' The two men walked across to the refreshments hall, to join Gurdeep and Sarah. Nothing else needed to be said.

They both knew in their hearts that *Sanctuary* would be filled again, with the sound of new travellers seeking a wilderness experience in the *Annapurna*. Some of them would be reflecting on the challenges they faced in their lives; seeking answers. And Alan would be looking down on them, smiling, when they arrived. He'd be hoping that they would absorb a little of what he had found there. What Luke and his flat-mates would never forget. In their beacon of hope: *Sanctuary*. A place between the mountains.

Gurdeep, Sarah and Luke sat quietly in their seats. The plane's engines roared into life, as the aircraft made its way across the air-strip. They would be leaving Nepal, in a few minutes. Each of them sat silently, alone with their thoughts. In his own mind, Luke was already planning to return in the new year. Thinking about the arrangements, helped to numb the pain of his loss.

Sarah pulled out some coins from her pocket to purchase a drink and immediately felt the smooth surface of the stone. It had lay there for several days. She pulled it out and stared at the gold- coloured word, etched across the rock: *alcohol.*

Thirty minutes elapsed before the carton of coffee arrived. Luke had expressed the need for something stronger and pulled the ring-top off the can of lager he had ordered. 'No wine for you Sarah?', he enquired.

'I don't think so, Luke. In fact, I'm going to give alcohol a rest for a while. After all, we can do without it, can't we?'

Gurdeep leaned across and cast a supporting nod in her direction.

'I certainly can,' she added, and I think, you can learn to do so, too'

Sarah had confided in Gurdeep, about her drinking habits. She described the damage her addiction had caused, both to herself and to those around her. Throughout the traumatic days they had spent together in Nepal, Gurdeep had begun to understand the enormity of her friend's challenge in dealing with this.

'Sarah, you are a strong character. You will conquer this,' she added.

'Maybe 'Sarah smiled. 'What about you, Gurdeep. Have you still got this?' She unclasped her hand to reveal the polished stone.

'Of course!' She fumbled around in her hand-bag and pulled out her own black pebble. Sarah didn't need to see the words inscribed upon the smooth rock. She had suspected that Gurdeep had been traumatised by a past relationship with a man, long before her testimony, at *Sanctuary*. 'I think it's time I tested my theory that men should be kept at a safe distance' she exclaimed. 'I might even start dating' she continued, 'maybe, sign up to an on-line site'

Sarah chuckled. 'Well, good luck with that one!'

Luke, meanwhile, spoke to the two women about his plans to return to Nepal. 'I want to help Amit with the work at *Sanctuary*, in memory of Saul, Alan and Dexa.'

They both said that they wanted to help, too, but needed time to deal with what had happened.

'Maybe, one day', Sarah sighed.

Gurdeep wasn't so sure. 'I think what Alan would have wanted most of all, for each of us, was to use this experience to strengthen our resolve. To meet the challenges we face, in our own lives, like he did, with renewed energy and wisdom. I'm certainly going to try!'

As the plane descended from the skies, towards Heathrow, the three friends promised to meet up at Saul's funeral service. After all, they needed to say goodbye to him, especially Luke. He had yet to compose the words that would convey how much he would miss him. There was some urgency in this, as Saul's family had asked if he could offer a short eulogy at the funeral. Saul may have been infuriating at times; arrogant, even a touch misogynistic, but he had been his best friend for as long as he could remember.

Beyond that day, they were all adamant about something else. It wouldn't be another ten years before they came together, again. Alan and Saul would never forgive them!

Thanks

My thanks go to Monica for her support and diligent reading of several drafts of the story. To Sue Gazey, for her time and efforts in proof-reading the text and to friends and members of the Oldswinford Writer's group, for their helpful comments at each stage of its development.

FICTION FROM APS BOOKS

(www.andrewsparke.com)

Andrew Sparke: *Abuse Cocaine & Soft Furnishings*

Andrew Sparke: *Copper Trance & Motorways*

HR Beasley: *Nothing Left To Hide*

Jean Harvey: *Pandemic*

Lee Benson: *So You Want To Own An Art Gallery*

Lee Benson: *Where's Your Art gallery Now?*

Michel Henri: *Mister Penny Whistle*

Michel Henri: *The Death Of The Duchess Of Grasmere*

Michael Harvey: *A Shattered Rose*

Nargis Darby: *A Different Shade Of Love*

Paul C. Walsh: *A Place Between The Mountains*